Presenting
Arthur Conan Doyle's Great Detective,

Sherlock Holmes

in

His Most Amazing Adventure—

The Red Poppy Menace

set in the Magical

Land of Oz,

based upon

the Original Classic Book Written by

L. Frank Baum,

with newly reported

Additions and Explanations by

Dr John H. Watson, M.D.

Sherlock Holmes in Oz

DISCOVERED BY
GARY LOVISI

ILLUSTRATED BY
LUCILLE CALI

WILDSIDE PRESS

Dedicated to The Brooklyn Munchkins:
Noah & Ryleigh
Elliott & Lucy

And of course,
Sir Arthur Conan Doyle
&
L. Frank Baum

Published by Wildside Press LLC.
wildsidepress.com | bcmystery.com

CHAPTER 1

The Red Poppy Menace

Sherlock Holmes was distraught, but he did not show it. That was not his way. He never showed his true emotions when working a problem, especially when something weighed deeply upon his mind. Something rather serious was bothering him now though, I could see it plainly, and it had to do with the Red Poppy Menace, as he called it. This was a newly potent strain of the purest form of opium, that had lately taken a hold of the populace in some of the poorer sections of London. And while use of this new drug was not spreading widely as yet, he was sure that it would spread far and wide once the supply increased. And with such a powerful drug, he knew it was just a matter of time before the supply increased—and the misery it caused. That was the nub for Holmes, he told me one evening in our rooms at Baker Street.

"Where is this drug coming from?" he asked contemplatively to himself, rather than directed at me, for I had no idea about it whatsoever. It was as if it were appearing from thin air!

A perplexing concern. And yet, I could see that there was something else upon his mind that troubled him, something perhaps entirely different?

"There is something else. What is it, Holmes?" I asked him upon that evening days ago. He was being his usual uncommunicative self, perhaps even more so this time, but upon that evening he did allow a few sparse words to escape his lips.

"I do not know what to make of it, Watson. Truly I do not. At least not yet. Do you remember Tonga?"

Of course I remembered him, way back from the case I had written about and entitled "The Sign of The Four." In fact, I had shot Tonga dead back then. I nodded bringing up the terrifying memory, "Ah, yes, that small bestial Andaman Island savage?"

"Well, that is what you wrote about him at the time in *The Strand*, you will recall, but I do not believe his origin was from that island at all, for I have been looking into that matter a bit more deeply lately. I have also been correlating information on a well-known crime set in Paris some years earlier, that was chronicled by the American writer, Edgar Allan Poe."

I looked over at Holmes inquiringly, then snapped my fingers in recognition, "Of course, I've got it! 'The Murders in the Rue Morgue'! A most famous mystery story by that talented American writer."

"Or was it merely a story? Was it indeed, fiction?" Holmes replied mysteriously. He looked at me carefully then told me, "In fact, the murders that took place in the Rue Morgue in Paris were based on a true account by Poe from 1834 of a 'monkey criminal'—apparently a trained baboon or some such creature—that was trained to steal. I wonder just what the creature was sent to steal."

I shook my head in disbelief. "That can not be. Of course the story was fiction. This is the other matter that preys upon your mind?"

"It is a investigation I am considering expanding. I have lately run across the most extraordinary small bestial fellow, and I am not at all sure what to make of him. Not yet. However, he reminds me of our old foe, Tonga. There is a definite resemblance, allowing for the passage of the years in his age, of course. It makes me wonder."

"What can he be then? Where can he be from?" I chimed in curious, wondering where my companion was going with this. "What of the one you said you encountered recently?"

"Oh, that fellow, he is long gone now, having escaped from me days ago. I am seeking him out still, but... I do not believe I will see him again, unless... "

"I am afraid I do not understand, Holmes."

My companion allowed a slim smile, "Well, neither do I yet, Watson, but let us drop this matter for the time being. The important subject at hand is this problem that has been termed by some as the 'Opium Zombies', also known with the acronym of 'O and Z', or just 'OZ', who have lately turned up in the poor sections of London."

"That is the red poppy problem, that you have told me about?"

"Correct, Watson, the Red Poppy Menace, and I fear it is a more dangerous situation than we have ever encountered before."

"And the matter of this bestial man you seek? Is this man connected with this red poppy business?"

Sherlock Holmes looked over at me and suddenly smiled broadly, actually appearing to exude some measure of joyfulness. I had seen his features appear similarly when making headway on a particularly difficult problem. He just looked directly at me and said rather surprisingly, "You know, good old Watson, while you may not be a great source of illumination—at times you can certainly be a powerful conductor of same."

I did not know what to make of this obtuse statement by my friend, but I knew he had given me one of his rare compliments and I was delighted by it. I looked at the Great Detective carefully, "What do you mean, Holmes?"

"Oh, nothing, Watson, nothing yet to speak of certainly, but I do believe you may have built a bridge for me in regard to these problems. I believe that soon we shall see how steady the planks you have set down prove to be."

"Bridge? Planks? I am afraid I am lost at sea here and do not know at all what you mean."

"Good, old Watson, fear not, when the time is right, I shall tell you all!"

* * * *

The two poor wretches in front of Sherlock Holmes sat locked in a cell in Scotland Yard. They stared blankly at the wall, unable to speak, or unwilling. He examined them most carefully and tried to engage them in conversation. Holmes soon realized that the men seemed to be under some strange form of outside mental control because of the power of this deadly new drug. It was most interesting and most vexing to the detective and myself as well. He could not get any answers from these men to the questions he needed to have answered, and I could see the frustration growing upon him.

Neither could Inspector Lestrade of Scotland Yard discover anything of merit from these men. He had lately been put in charge of the case representing the official police. It was most strange. Most vexing for us all to behold.

I could see that the two men Holmes examined were both recent victims of the use of the mysterious red poppy powder, some unknown derivative of opium, no doubt, and yet something entirely new that had never been seen before. It had lately and suddenly shown up in some areas of the great city, among certain of the lower classes of the populace. These users each seemed to be linked to some network which all seemed to be under the control of the person who supplied them with the red powder. His grip upon them, and the power of the drug over them, seemed almost complete. They were whispered by some to be 'Opium Zombies'. Opium in some sections of the city of London had become a plague, but this drug seemed even worse.

These drug users would readily admit to Holmes and the police, the power and attraction the drug held for them, but they would not under any circumstances divulge any information about who the seller or sellers of the drug were. They would not—*or could not*—speak of where they had obtained the drug, which in itself was most unusual. In my experience with Holmes I have learned that criminals generally enjoy talking, and even bragging about their crimes, for reasons of ego certainly, but also to make a deal with the police for lighter treatment. Not in this case. In all likelihood I imagined they did not know the intimate details, however, someone had to know where this drug was originating.

It proved to be a most uncanny situation, and the users appeared to be under the most complete control by a drug that Holmes had ever seen set upon any human being—and he was an expert on the various drugs used during our day—legal and illegal. I also agreed with him, being a medical man, my knowledge of all types of drugs was vast. I could see this conundrum filled my friend with great concern, for Sherlock Holmes realized the incredible danger the Red Poppy Menace would cause if it's use spread wider among the populace. And he was certain that such a powerful and alluring drug would definitely spread far and wide—or as far as the supply would take it. For the hundredth time he wondered how great the supply of the drug here in London might be, and where it was coming from. That concerned Holmes greatly because it seemed impossible to find out the answer to this most crucial question.

Sherlock Holmes told me, "I have already investigated the opium dens and other nefarious places in the East End since the drug first appeared a week or so ago, as well as the cribs and hell houses in the most dangerous sections of our city such as Limehouse and Whitechapel, but I came away with little information. However, the little I have discovered astounded me. The allure of the drug among it's users seems all-powerful and complete. The use of it, even one time, binds the user to it as a devoted slave. Slaves, who of late are involved in various criminal activities. Even some law-abiding citizens with no criminal record newly involved with the drug, will do anything, and stop at nothing, to obtain another chance at indulgence. This drug could prove to be an extremely dangerous plague throughout London, and eventually England. It must be stopped. I reported these facts to Lestrade who has lately been placed in charge of the official police in-vestigation, much to his dismay."

Lestrade just shook his head in frustration.

I looked at my friend, "It does seem to be a serous problem. I have never seen anything like it."

"Nor have I seen anything like it, and I can assure you that means quite a lot, for I have seen everything related to drugs of all types, as you know," Holmes repeated to the Yard man and myself in a simple statement of fact. A fact I could see he was not willing to accept.

"Neither have I, Mr. Holmes," Lestrade added grimly, and the little Yarder shook his head sadly. "The victims appear as if under some all-consuming trance, rather than the usual drugs we are familiar with, they seem as if under some almost otherworldly power. They crave the drug above all things and it seems to strip the very humanity out of them. Look at them! They just sit there as if waiting to be told what to do. To be com-manded! But by who? I have never seen anything quite like it. I should not admit this, but... it almost seems to me as if they are held sway by some dark magical power. Ensorcelled!"

I looked at Homes. He nodded gently, spoke up softly, "Yes, I have heard the term 'Opium Zombies' used by your men, sometimes shortened to the acronym of 'OZ', but I am sure we are not dealing with anything supernatural here."

"I am not so sure, Mr. Holmes."

"Oh, come now, Lestrade, let us not exaggerate the matter and travel down that dark and dreary road. I know you feel you must go as far and wide in stating to me your theory on the possibilities on this mystery, do you not? But please, do not go too far a field," Holmes told the inspector sharply. Then he looked at him and spoke up softly, "At least not yet. We have much ado with the natural course of crime and criminality—so supernatural agencies need not apply. In matters such as these, I fear there is more Moriarity than magic to this problem."

"Aye, but he is long dead, Mr. Holmes," Lestrade reminded us with a sharp look upon his face.

I looked to Holmes but he did not answer the Inspector's question, instead he continued on a different tack.

"What we must do, is find the origin of this drug—the source," my companion told the inspector sharply. "That will solve our problem and answer all our questions."

"Well, I admit I am stumped. We do not know what to do about it here at the Yard," Lestrade readily admitted rather distraught.

"Neither do I, at least for the moment," Holmes reluctantly agreed, and the fact was obviously annoying him greatly. I could see he was thinking the problem through on multiple levels and I felt he was coming up with some rather surprising possibilities. I felt that he saw the facts pointing in a direction he was not ready to take. Not yet.

Lestrade continued, "Well, we know the drug is extremely dangerous, even deadly. The victims are incapable of furnishing me and my men the information we seek. It is almost as if they are under some type of mental compulsion that I am not able to comprehend or break through. Something that controls the mind. Hypnotism, perhaps? Mayhap some type of magic? I know it all sounds rather like a great humbug, but I can not explain it."

"Surely not hypnotism. Who would hypnotize these poor wretches? And for what reason? And as for magic? Really, Lestrade! No, it is not any of that, but a medical evaluation might help. I have brought Watson in on this problem, even though he has a rather personal family situation at the moment that is commanding all of his attention."

"I am ready and willing to do anything that I can to help," I told the two detectives.

"Well, I suppose a medical man might aid us in this inquiry, but honestly, Mr. Holmes, I do not think anything can help us get any answers from these beastly users," Lestrade spoke up very much concerned.

"While there are only a few cases I have seen of this Red Poppy Menace, from what I have seen, I tend to agree with you Lestrade, at least in part," Holmes stated giving me a slim but thoughtful grin. "The red powder is coming from somewhere, being brought into the city and distributed at the usual places, by many of the usual people in the criminal underworld, and by smugglers, but where is it originating? Not from the usual places, that is for certain. Your men have looked everywhere. It is not being brought into London on any ship, or train, and not by dray wagon. Your men have checked all those conveyances most thoroughly. There is something we are missing and it is a crucial key to this entire scheme."

"What can it be, Mr. Holmes?"

"Indeed! As yet, I do not have a workable theory upon the problem. You know it is not my way to theorize without facts, and we are missing too many significant ones at the moment for me to even surmise what this might all be about. More investigation and more evidence is required before we can act."

"Well, I am at a loss as to what to do about it," Lestrade admitted reluctantly for I was sure now that he was getting pressure from his higher ups at the Yard on this case. That was why the inspector had rushed over to Baker Street the day before to ask the famed consulting detective to intercede in a case that had him fully stumped. Holmes thought long and hard but said nothing. I could see that the case had him stumped as well, and that very fact rankled him immensely. I knew that he felt it should not be that difficult a case to solve, yet it was most perplexing, for it seemed to be a problem without a solution.

I was also perplexed by what I had seen and learned about this deadly drug.

"What is to be done, Mr. Holmes?" Lestrade pleaded now. "If this—this devilish contagion—well, if it spreads throughout the city... ?"

"Then London is doomed. This red poppy powder is more powerful than anything we have ever encountered," Holmes told us in dire warning, then he rubbed his long chin, nodded carefully. "The origin of this deadly powder must be from some remote and distant land indeed, but I know not where. Perhaps Asia or darkest Africa? And yet... it can not be. For I am familiar with every type of drug upon the market and every point of origin for every type of drug from around the world. This is certainly coming from somewhere, but it seems to be originating from a new source we have never encountered before. That in itself is most unusual. Certainly unique. It may even be—impossible. I know that premise sounds incredible—but what we may believe is impossible, is only impossible, until it is made to become—*possible*."

Lestrade looked at Holmes skeptically, "I am afraid I do not understand you, Mr. Holmes."

Holmes allowed a slim smile, "Just thinking out loud, Lestrade. Just thinking out loud. I have always found that whenever you eliminate all extraneous factors, whatever remains, however fantastic, must be the truth."

"What do you mean by that?" I asked in a low whisper. I wondered what Holmes might be implying, but as I had already told him, I had more serious personal matters upon my mind just then. Matters of a rather serious family problem.

"There seems more to this Red Poppy Menace—*much more*—than meets the eye or even the dark confines of the minds of it's hapless users," Holmes said softly, then in a whisper he added, "I fear the users are becoming more violent. The desire for the drug is too strong, causing them to do anything to obtain the red powder. Crime is up, the streets are becoming dangerous, the drug is causing the criminal threat to expand as never before. Should this trend continue, our city—civilization itself—may be in danger!"

Lestrade nodded, and looked for some further answer or explanation from the man many called The Great Detective, who was also my friend and companion, but Holmes would say no more at the moment.

Sherlock Holmes quickly took his leave of the Inspector, and he and I headed back to Baker Street. I could tell that he had many deep thoughts weighing upon his mind concerning this unique problem and they were proving to be of a most disturbing nature.

CHAPTER 2: A GIRL HAS GONE MISSING

"Something always interesting occurs whenever I travel to America," Sherlock Holmes told me the next morning. It was in late October.

I noted his words but did not reply right away, for I had serious matters upon my mind just then. Nevertheless, I wondered just what he was thinking about now. What did he mean about America? Why mention that subject here and now?

"Oh, come now, Watson, tell me what it is that has you in such a funk, sulking about our rooms like a visitor at a Welsh wake?"

"So you noticed?" I replied somewhat morosely.

"Hah, it does not take any special powers of observation to read you, my friend. So tell me, out with it now! What is it that is bothering you? I know it has something to do with the news in a recent telegram you received from America," Holmes told me with a confident tone of voice. I was immediately touched by his concern, but how did he know about the telegram? I never told him about it, and I had not shown it to him, nor divulged it's most singular contents.

"It is... Well... Dorothy. She is gone. She has apparently gone missing without a trace."

"Ah, yes, your wife's great-niece over in America. I see."

"Yes... "

"Serious?"

"I do not know, but I am afraid that it is."

"Well that certainly sounds serious enough for me. So you want to travel to America to help search for her?"

"Well, yes, I do—I mean—well, I cannot leave you now, not with this Red Poppy Menace taking a hold here in London. It is all you talk about."

"I know."

"And then there is that little bestial man who you are seeking," I added thoughtfully, "I fear he means you harm."

"Perhaps, and he may prove a most interesting problem. Together with him, and a rather sudden and unknown influx of a deadly drug, things may be coming to a head soon," Holmes told me with a grim look.

I nodded sadly, "Terrible, it is simply dreadful."

"Well?" he prompted.

I looked at Holmes closely, then he came out with it. "Yes, I am thinking of taking my leave for America, and that is why I did not desire to burden you with knowledge of, what is after all, a family matter—nor ask for your help if I went out on my own and took ship to America. You are much too busy now, and your presence much too valuable here in London."

"Never so busy, nor so valuable, as to help you, Watson. Your problem is my problem," Holmes told me in a soft warm voice that touched me more than I wanted to admit.

"Thank you."

Then he looked at me firmly and a faraway look came to his eyes. "You know I am somewhat loath to travel back to America since my earlier adventure there. It was before your time, good Watson, in my early days with Doctor Bell. That did not turn out so well for me, but I am older now and hopefully somewhat wiser, and I have had a yen to see America once again before old age creeps up upon me and makes such travel impossible. Indeed, I would like to see the 'states' as they call them, one more time. A most fascinating country. I propose we sail to New York City and from there take a train directly to this Kansas place."

"How ever did you know about Kansas?" I asked astonished, for I had not told my companion any of this information. And while he knew my wife had a great niece over in America, named Dorothy, that was all he knew, for I had never told him much about her, nor where she lived.

"Really ,Watson, your problems, and even your feelings, are an open book to me. They prey upon my mind, just as they do upon your own mind. I can hardly not take notice. I see you in distress over this problem, and it disturbs me greatly, so I desire to help you and your wife's young grand niece," Holmes told me in a soft tone, his voice and manner so sincere his offer of aid touched me deeply.

"Well, thank you again, Holmes," I responded softly, trying to hold my emotions in check. Here was a true-blue friend if ever I needed one! I was most happy that he would be my traveling companion to America. I was also relieved that our travels would take us out of London, and him away from any danger from that small bestial man who appeared to be following him. "When shall we leave?"

"Why, the sooner the better, my old friend. I know you desire to leave immediately. In fact, I have taken the liberty of securing for us two tickets on the new *S.S. Britannia*, destined for New York, which is leaving from Liverpool later today. So prepare your things quickly, we must depart at once to catch our train to the coast and board our ship in time. Then it is across the wide Atlantic to New York. From New York we will make use of the American railway system to take us into the heartland of that nation, to that place called Kansas. The game is afoot, Watson! Are you ready?"

"You know that I am, Holmes, and thank you. You are so…well, thank you."

"Think nothing of it, old man."

"But I do think of it. I feel I am being remiss with you in my selfish needs. Should you leave London now? At this time? You will be leaving our great city unguarded," I stated, suddenly feeling rather guilty, as if I was the cause of Holmes deserting our city and his important detective work at such a crucial time. "What will happen here without you to stop the acts of the criminal class? And what of this Red Poppy Menace?"

"Nonsense, we have time yet with them. Lestrade, that little bulldog, is busy on the case, and Scotland Yard should be able to hold the line until we return. I can not allow my Boswell to go upon such a taxing and dangerous mission alone, so far from home, without my full support. In any event, it will do me good to get away from London for a time, air out my thoughts on this red poppy matter, and that other thing, and it will do my heart good to help you with your problem—as you have aided me so many times with my own, Watson."

"You are a true-blue friend, and yet... Is there something you are withholding from me, Holmes?" I asked him plainly, for this seemed so sudden, I felt that perhaps he may have had some ulterior motive in his accompanying me upon my trip to America.

"No, not at all," he replied simply with a slight grin that I thought rather mischievous, but without any evidence to the contrary, nor any other explanation, I took him at his word.

"Well, then, I thank you very much," I said softly, holding my emotions in check, even as I had the nagging feeling that something else was up with his decision to leave London at this time and come with me to America. He knew something—or suspected something—I was sure. I just wondered what it might be. However since he was not forthcoming upon the matter, I let it drop. In fact, he had denied everything when later I questioned him about it, so I put my paltry suspicions on the side and forgot about them for the moment. Instead, I would concentrate upon the problem at hand, my niece Dorothy, and locating her whereabouts. That was what pressed firmly upon my thoughts, for I feared greatly for her safety.

"Then let us be off at once!" Holmes told me in an excited voice, "To America!"

"Yes, at once!" I replied, and we quickly packed a few things and instantly made ready to leave Baker Street.

CHAPTER 3: OUR TRAVEL TO AMERICA

I will not bore you gentle reader with the steamship and railway trip to far off America, to bustling New York City, and then into the interior of the vast American continent, all the way to the faraway state of Kansas.

It proved to be a long and uneventful journey for the most part, dry and dirty, lonely and hot, but Holmes used it to wring out of me all of the particulars of my nagging problem. It was quite a conundrum. My wife's great niece had gone missing—not missing as if having run-away, or even having been abducted or kidnapped—as terrible as that would be—but missing as if a veritable supernatural force had simply snatched her off the face of the Earth. I do not know why I felt this way but it seemed to me to be the only explanation I could come up with at the time from the news I had heard from Kansas. It seemed an incredible event. The telegram I had received about the situation from our American side of my family was most perplexing and incomprehensible. I did not know what to make of it, but when I showed Holmes the telegram he just nodded sagely. He did not so much as take it from my hand to give it a closer look. That was most unlike him. I wondered why, then I soon discovered the answer.

"I must admit, I have already read the telegram, Watson. When you were out before we left London, I took a little peak," he told me in a soft rather sly tone.

"A little peak, Holmes!" I chided him gently, surprised by his action, but not really angry. Actually I was rather touched that he cared so much about my problem to break his rigid rules of decorum and privacy in an effort to discover what was bothering me so deeply.

"I had to do it, Watson. I could not allow you to sulk around our rooms in London forever. I had to know what was in that message. And now that I do, I am sure we are doing the right thing. That is why I immediately secured our travel plans, even before I spoke to you about leaving London."

"Holmes, I do not know what to say."

"Then tell me this, Henry and Emily have taken on the role of parents to Dorothy. Are they good people? From sound stock? Are they prone to hysterics?" Holmes asked me carefully.

"Hysterics, absolutely not. Not at all. They are the best and most down-to-earth people you could ever meet. Solid Rocks of Gibraltar, I say. Yet, they are poor hardscrabble farmers, but good Christians and entirely devoted to Dorothy," I told him firmly.

"Just so. I just wanted to hear it from your own lips. That is why this telegram raised in me so many causes for concern."

"How so, Holmes?" I asked, feeling a nagging fear about not having seen something in that message, that he saw. I wondered just what my companion saw in that message, that I had missed? As if reading my very thoughts, he spoke up firmly.

"You know, that I read between the lines, Watson." Holmes told me simply, explaining his methods. "There is much here not written. Sometimes what is *not* written in such a message can be just as important—or even *more* important—than what *is* written. I am afraid that I can not explain more than that at this time."

I did not know what to make of this cryptic statement. What did he fear? I could see that he grew more and more intrigued by my problem, and I could tell that he was positively chomping at the bit to begin his investigation the closer our train took us to Kansas. I also began to wonder, once again, if Holmes had some ulterior motive for helping me in my journey to find my niece, for I had some inkling that there was more to this journey for him than met the eye.

If, in fact, Holmes had any theory upon the matter, he was loath to discuss it with me at that time, which I knew after our long association was ever his way on any current investigation. Nevertheless, I had the unfathomable feeling that there was somehow a connection between my problem, and perhaps Holmes' investigation into the Red Poppy Menace. Of course, I had no idea whatever that might be.

Perhaps, the thought came to me, that Holmes had some indication that the drug may have originated in America? I did not know what to make of that. I shook my head in consternation, for I could not understand it. It did not seem possible that the drug originated in America at all. Regardless, I did not share these thoughts with Holmes, as I knew he would not elaborate on any theory he held on the matter just then, if he in fact, had any theory on the matter at all. I knew he would tell me—what he wanted to tell me—in his own good time. So I decided to wait patiently, making friendly conversation and enjoying the beautiful scenery of our long journey. We rode briskly by rail through America. I hoped to see some of the colorful wild Indians I had heard tell about as we traveled farther West, but none were in our vision. However, we did see some of the amazing natural wonders of the land. America is truly a lovely country blessed by God.

We spent most of our time sleeping, eating, and reading. A lot of reading. The reading time was well spent. I enjoyed one of Doyle's rousing historical adventure novels, *The White Company*, while Holmes spent his time reading some mysterious manuscript of unbound sheets of paper.

"I say, Holmes, what is that you are reading?" I asked him curious, while I watched him peruse his sheets of paper silently, nodding his head in agreement with what the author had written. It was obvious he was enjoying it quite a bit.

"It is a manuscript that Professor Edward Challenger presented to me for his new book one week ago. I have just gotten around to reading it now. It is entitled, *Cyclones and Violent Atmospheric Disturbances*. It is a most interesting study of extreme weather patterns."

"I must confess I have never heard of that particular volume by the Professor," I replied, for while everyone had heard of Challenger, a most difficult man to deal with, he was a brilliant scientist. I, like many of us who were well-read, always tried to buy a copy of the newest Challenger book to appear on the book stalls. Holmes and I had never met the great man as of yet, but we hoped to do so some day.

"A most fascinating work and likely it will never see publication. It is quite controversial, Watson."

"Yes, as is the Professor himself, I am sure. Well, I certainly hope we never meet up with any of that violent weather you have told me about."

Holmes only smiled, "Well, actually, old friend, I hope that we do. In his book Challenger posits certain fantastical atmospheric actions that our vaulted scientific heads would never countenance."

"I see, and what do you think about what he says?"

"There seems to be much merit to his suppositions and arguments, but I believe we shall see soon if his theories prove correct or not, my friend. Kansas is a known attractor of these violent weather disturbances."

"How so?" I asked Holmes carefully. I certainly hoped we never encountered any such powerful storm as a cyclone, but Holmes had now gone silent upon the subject, and knowing his ways, I sighed and continued delving deeper into my Doyle novel. Meanwhile our train rumbled onward through the wild American countryside.

We debarked at the Topeka train station less than a week from the day we had left London. Our travel had been the fastest possible, due to Holmes' magnificent ability to match the logistics of travel to the maximum efficiency and speed that was possible by our modern conveyances of travel. Holmes had timed the logistics of our journey perfectly, to ensure our quickest passage. He had told me that while time was of the essence, we still had a certain amount of days before things would come to a head. I had no idea what he might mean by such a statement, and he did not elaborate upon it to me either. I assumed he knew what he was doing though, and I was just relieved that he was with me on this trip.

Kansas proved to be a great flat land that stretched out seemingly forever in every direction and is crowned by tall golden wheat fields and green cattle pastures. And a lot of cows. It is an amazing place, but far too desolate for my liking after living so long in the teaming city of London. I am sure that difference had a similar effect upon Holmes.

We left Topeka and hired a wagon with a large trustworthy horse—it was a small wagon that carried ourselves, some food, and our two small valises of clothing and personal items quite well. The wagon was called by the very American name, 'buckboard', though I had no idea what the word meant.

Holmes and I soon traversed the roads in our buckboard that American frontier settlers must have used to travel on their way out West decades before. Holmes and I took turns driving the dray horse that pulled our buckboard far into the vast Kansas farmland country.

"It appears to me that we may be traveling the same road that many an intrepid American frontiersmen did decades ago, Watson," Holmes told me with a light laugh. "A rather unique experience, is it not?"

"Yes, I can not believe I am riding in this buckboard of all things, and here in the middle of the vast American West of all places on Earth. I almost feel like one of those American cowboys, Holmes, a cowboy straight out from London."

"Yet no Indians in sight," Holmes told me with a grin.

"I know, I had hoped to see some of these red savages, that the Americans so often write about."

"Hah, savages, you say, Watson? We are all capable of savagery under certain circumstances, but let us travel on. I am sure we shall reach our destination soon."

We headed to a stark corner of the state where the county that was our destination was located. It was there that the farm was located where my great niece had mysteriously gone missing. We reached the farm the next morning, a vast flat land of tall grass and prickly scrub. There was a stable, fences and a silo, but no house visible.

At the farm we met Henry and Emily who were Dorothy's uncle and aunt. They appeared to be wonderful, friendly, solid people. They were living in a large tent at the time, engaged in rebuilding their farmhouse, which recently had been taken in a massive cyclone.

Once the greetings were over with, at my companion's prodding they joined in to tell Holmes and myself the story of what had happened to Dorothy as we sat in a partially built section of the new home. The house was just a shell really, not yet rebuilt. The original home had been totally taken up and away by the massive cyclone that had hit the farm some weeks ago. Uncle Henry and Aunt Em had saved their lives by seeking refuge in a deep root cellar that they had dug under the house for just such massive storms. The husband and wife were saved, but not Dorothy, nor her little dog. They were still missing.

"So tell me all that happened here," Holmes asked the elderly couple, looking from face to face intently. "And leave out no detail, however small or inconsequential it may seem to be."

"It all happened during the storm, Mr. Holmes," Uncle Henry explained with a deep grimace. "It was a regular terror, a bad one, and it come upon us sudden-like, as they tend to do around these parts. My wife and I had to run immediately into the root cellar for safety. There was no time for anything else. At times like this, mere seconds can be precious. There was much confusion. Even panic. You have no idea the destruction such storms can do and they put the fear and terror into all who live hereabouts. Kansas has been cursed by such terrible storms. In all the confusion we did not see Dorothy. I surely thought her already safe in the cellar, as I had always impressed upon her during such storms. I discovered she was missing when I went into the cellar, and such was the full fury of the storm I could not go out and look for her. For either my wife or I to leave then and look for Dorothy in that raging storm, would have meant a death sentence. I assumed then that Dorothy must be in her room, in our farmhouse. I prayed she would be safe there. So we had no choice but to wait the storm out and hope for the best."

"After the storm passed," Aunt Em continued barely holding back her tears now, "The entire house was gone! It was incredible! Good Lord! Henry and I ran out from the root cellar and combed all the land far and wide to find Dorothy. We feared for the worse, but we found nothing. No body was ever found, not even her little dog. It was most unusual. There was no sign of her at all, or the dog—or even the house."

"Your house—or the remains of it—were never found?" Holmes asked curiously.

"That is the strange thing about it all, Mr. Holmes. Nothing at all was ever found, not any beams or even splinters of wood," Henry stated sadly.

Sherlock Holmes nodded grimly, "There should be some wreckage of the house hereabouts. There should also be a body found somewhere after such a violent storm. The fact that there was nothing found... well... It is a most intriguing case. Your Dorothy may, in fact, still be alive, somewhere. There is always hope."

"I am sure that she is alive," Aunt Em stated. "Somewhere."

Holmes nodded thoughtfully, then added, "These intense storms have always held a fascination for me, their raw power, the furious energy of nature surely make them something to be feared. These are incredible natural phenomena and they are worthy of further investigation. There is no pretty way to say this, but they have been known to hurl bodies many miles away. So have you looked far and wide?"

"We have searched far and wide, Mr. Holmes, my wife and I, and everyone in the county is looking for Dorothy, but she has not shown up, alive or dead," Uncle Henry stated, then he looked down, sadly, adding, "Not even a body, poor girl. Or even the remains of our house! Nothing."

Aunt Em muffled a cry and shed more tears at the very thought of her young ward missing and presumed dead.

"Well, Watson, the immense power these storms contain, their massive energy, I do not doubt that under the proper conditions they might propel someone a very great distance indeed."

"Such has been proven over and over again by these storms," Uncle Henry added. "However, we have searched everywhere to no avail."

Holmes nodded with a peculiar glint in his eyes, "Yes, I am sure, far and wide they might range, indeed. Then we must look even farther and wider."

"What are you getting at, Holmes?" I asked my friend curiously.

"Ah, nothing just yet, Watson. Nothing at this time, but we must keep an open mind, even as we work to dig out more facts. Let me ask you both, is there anyone that Dorothy would seek refuge with during such a storm? If she could not get into the root cellar, suppose she came there late and found the door was locked, then where might she go for safety?"

"The storm cellar of course. That is where we go," Uncle Henry stated, then rubbing his head he looked at Holmes, "but there is something else."

"Yes, and what might that be?" Holmes asked immediately interested.

"I believe she was last seen with the Professor," Aunt Em suddenly spoke up. "She sometimes visited that young man who calls himself a Professor. He says he is a writer, a newspaperman, and sometimes even a magician. He tells fortunes and such around the county. He lives near here and was at the County Fair. She may have went to see him—but seeing the weather that day, it may be doubtful she went there."

Holmes darted a look at the old woman indicating for her to continue.

"And what else?" Holmes prompted the older man.

"Ah, Mr. Holmes, I guess Cousin John did not exaggerate your powers. Yes, there is something else," Aunt Em continued. "We also heard this Professor is said to be missing a relative—a fellow who also disappeared without a trace!"

"I see," Sherlock Holmes replied thoughtfully, patiently waiting.

Uncle Henry suddenly brightened up, said, "Yep, that's gotta be it, I recall there was that wagon of the Professor close by."

"So who is this Professor?" Holmes asked eagerly, fully attentive now.

"Why, Professor Wonder The Mysterious, he calls himself. He's a magician, but also I believe something of a confidence man from the circus, from Omaha. The children are drawn to him because of his reciting such fantastic stories and wondrous tales. I have no idea where he hears of such things! He has quite the imagination. He lives in the vicinity," Uncle Henry added.

"Yes, that is it!" Aunt Em spoke up sharply now.

"Professor Wonder?" I asked, trying to imagine who this mysterious person might be and what connection he had with my missing niece, Dorothy. I looked towards Holmes with a grim shake of my head. I was sure that the man was just some recalcitrant drummer or mountebank, or a patent medicine salesman and perhaps slippery scoundrel, no doubt. Not a real Professor, and certainly not a doctor. I thought such a man could not be a person who would be of interest to us. However, Holmes, did not agree.

"Yes, I see, and that is most interesting," Holmes said quietly, then with firm determination he looked at me and added, "Well then, Watson, we must seek out this Professor Wonder immediately."

CHAPTER 4: THE MARVELOUS PROFESSOR WONDER

Uncle Henry and Aunt Em had indeed come through with the information we needed and told us the best location to find this mysterious Professor. Holmes and I quickly hitched up our horse to our buckboard and were soon on the way to seek out and discover what we could from this Professor Wonder, the magician out of Omaha. We had learned that he was connected with the County Fair and now lived in a local area about two miles from the Vale Farm, so we made our way there.

The two of us had taken our small wagon and drove it quickly through the flat scrubland to the Professor's home. The land was low and relatively flat so it was not so difficult for Holmes, or myself, to drive our light wagon. Our trusty horse moved at a steady gait, more of a trot than a run, which was just fine with me.

The ride out there took another twenty minutes, but it was pleasant enough in the cool morning air of Kansas.

I saw his homestead straight away, but he also had what looked like some type of drummers wagon hitched nearby. How could I miss it? It was large and most gaily painted in amazingly bright and vibrant—even garish—colors, showing fantastic mythical images of all manner of animals that were accompanied by the most melodramaticly descriptive words painted in elaborate colorful cursive script.

Wonder The Marvelous!
Seated at the Throne of Ozma, Queen Zixi of Ix!
The amazing Rinkitink!
Famed author of 'The Maid of Arran'!
Visions of the mysterious Red Poppy!
From the Land of Little Men!

I had no idea of what any of this might mean.
In large lettering it also modestly proclaimed:

The Mysterious Miranda Can Answer all Your Questions!

Indeed!
Then there was this:

Let Him Read Your Past, Present and Futur
in His Magical Crystal Ball!

It was quite a bit much for me to take in, but to say that I was intrigued was no lie. However, I could never believe any of this fancy verbiage and the wild images that to me were the worst examples of just sheer dumb thumb twaddle. I grew a bit testy as I drove our buckboard closer. After all, I was a medical man, a man of science, and this type of mystical flummery annoyed me no end, and was something most men of science abhorred.

I looked to Holmes and he just gave me a curious grin but he said nothing. I however, would not be so silent upon the matter.

"It is obvious to me this man must be some kind of despicable charlatan and perhaps he may even be dangerous. I fear for my poor niece if she has fallen into his clutches," I whispered to Holmes as we approached the location of the Professor's camp. I carefully let my hand move to my revolver, where it was secreted in my coat pocket.

"We shall see, Watson, we shall see. Well, hello now, it seems we have arrived at the Professor's homestead."

"Yes we are there," I admitted to my friend a bit petulantly.

"Say nothing to this man, Watson," Holmes told me in a low warning tone as our horse pulled our conveyance into the Professor's homestead. His wagon and an amazing colorful hot air balloon were nearby. "Let me do all the talking for now."

I nodded, and drove our buckboard up closer to the house. Then I suddenly saw Professor Wonder. I looked him over carefully noting that he seemed to be a rather elegant and young gent dressed in formal black clothing with a high hat and much looking his part as a man of learning and knowledge. He had dark hair pasted down and parted in the center of his head, and a thick dark mustache. His eyes then drew my attention, for they seemed to twinkle with delight and some wonderment. I could not help but instantly take a liking to such a grand-looking fellow and realized that perhaps my earlier assumptions about him might have been a bit premature.

"Professor Wonder?" Holmes inquired of the man as he disembarked our wagon and quickly strode over to where the man was busy attending his camp fire. I tied up our horse and then joined Holmes straightaway. The Professor had something boiling in a pot over the flames.

"Ah, yes, I am most certainly him!" the man replied in an easy friendly manner with light joyful laughter. His eyes twinkled with delight. It was obvious he was happy to receive our company—or any company. "And whom do I have the honor of addressing?"

"I am Sherlock Holmes, and this is my friend, Doctor John Watson."

"Not the famous Sherlock Holmes from London? Can it be? Why, I know of you! I have actually read some stories about your famous cases in *The Strand Magazine*! You know we get them here in the States as well, and being an actor and newspaperman myself—among other things—I am aware of current and popular personages of note," the Professor replied with a wide smile of instant joy. His eyes lit up with a bright twinkle as his rather bushy dark eyebrows positively bristled. "I believe the stories were narrated by a doctor? Is he that fellow? Surely it must be him! This is wonderful, a magnificent meeting and so unexpected. I wonder what it could be about? Are you investigating a criminal case?"

Holmes remained silent, but allowed a light smile.

I nodded with a grin, it was pleasant and surprising to be recognized for my writings so far from home and to hear such ebullient praise. No matter the source.

Holmes then spoke up modestly, "The stories are the work of my most able biographer here, the good doctor."

"Well, well, this is truly wonderful! Imagine meeting the two of you all the way out here! Amazing, simply amazing! Well, you are most welcome here! Both of you!" the Professor said giving us each a winning smile. I was curious as to what he was a professor of, but did not ask him. "It is so good to meet you both—but what the heck are you doing out here in the wilds of Kansas of all places?"

"I am afraid that is a long story," I spoke up, in spite of Holmes admonition to me not to speak.

Holmes looked at me sharply and I nodded, accepting his mild rebuke.

"Well, come on over here, it is so good to meet you both," the Professor told us as he offered his hand in a welcoming handshake to Holmes and I which we shook with aplomb. It was a hearty, purposeful grip from a man of substance. "Would you like some coffee? The water is almost on the boil. Or should I offer you gents some tea, you both being Britishers?"

"No, thank you, Professor," Holmes replied as his sharp eyes looked over the camp and the area around his home most closely. "We are seeking some information."

"And what might that be about?"

"The Vale girl, Dorothy, she is Doctor Watson's great niece," Holmes stated simply.

Professor Wonder shook his head sadly. "Ah, yes, Dorothy—lovely child—strong-willed. I told her to get back home as soon as she could, the wind kicked up so quickly. The girl finally decided to make her way back home."

"Then you saw her!" I blurted.

Holmes gave me a sharp look.

"Oh sure, right before the big cyclone hit. The winds were up and would soon grow to a raging fury. I knew it would be a big one. I was battening down my house and wagon and hoping to ride out the storm here—which I did. I remember feeling badly for the girl and hoping she made it back safely. Did she?"

"She has disappeared," I stated grimly.

"Oh, I am so sorry. She was a most charming child."

"So she told you she was going back home?" Holmes asked carefully.

"Yes."

"I see," Holmes responded thoughtfully.

"Was she taken up into the cyclone?" the Professor then asked with a dark look.

"We do not know, but no body has yet been found." Holmes stated looking at the Professor most carefully and thoughtfully.

"Poor girl, but if she was sucked up into the vortex—she may have been sent—anywhere... She too could be anywhere at all," the Professor added rather mysteriously.

"Possibly," Holmes admitted, then added, "but what exactly do you mean by that? By... anywhere?"

Professor Wonder sighed, thought deeply for a long moment, "Well, it is a theory I have. As Professor Wonder living here in Kansas, I have seen many strange and mysterious things. These Kansas cyclones possess immense power that could send anyone sucked upwards into the vortex very great distances. Usually for their determent. However, the nature of the cyclone is almost by arbitrary design. Why, I have witnessed complete destruction next to absolute and utter peace. Amazing! I have also discovered that there is a central core of the cyclone vortex, an eye in essence, that is very stable and calm, if you can believe such a thing possible? If she somehow was flung into that area by the high winds, she too could have been sent... Well, who knows where? I know of this type of thing before—when a person went missing during a storm and no body has been found. Perhaps I should put the question to my crystal ball?"

"Crystal ball?" I asked in evident surprise.

"Yes, I think you should," Holmes said with a speedy reply that surprised me. I was sure he must have been thinking of the theories he had recently read from Challenger's book, and that those theories seemed to agree with what the Professor was telling us. It seemed most strange, but even more so because of the Professor's mentioning his crystal ball.

I looked at my detective friend with open skepticism now. Was he seriously considering allowing this mountebank charlatan to consult a crystal ball of all things to answer our questions concerning Dorothy?

Holmes just nodded, "Please do so, Professor."

"Then I shall do just that," the Professor told my companion, "please follow me inside."

I shook my head back and forth in confusion.

Holmes merely smiled and said, "Yes, Professor, that would be most interesting if you could find some information for us on Dorothy, through your spiritual contrivances."

"I would be delighted to help you, Mr. Holmes, if I and Miranda are able to do so," the Professor replied and with that he led us into the back of his small home, which was lavishly furnished with his living accommodations. Inside he had quite a full and busy living area. He deftly seated us around a table upon which in the center, sat a large clear glass or crystal globe held in place by a strange clawed hand that functioned as some kind of stand. It looked very old, even ancient.

I immediately noticed Holmes' eyes quickly scanning the device, and the living space around us most carefully. He seemed to notice two—what seemed to me to be mountebank wizard hats—high-pointed, large-brimmed affairs colorfully decorated with stars and other mystical symbols that were hung from a wall, but he spoke no words about them. It was most strange to me. Holmes also seemed fascinated by an old daguerreotype of two young boys, brothers obviously, dressed as magicians, with one appearing to be the Professor in his childhood days. There were also toy guns and toy soldiers, and two wooden riding horses for small children, all neatly preserved. I wondered about that, but the Professor did not make any comment when he saw my friend looking around his living quarters, nor did Holmes ask him any questions about these items at the time. I wondered why.

I was about to ask Holmes to comment upon his observations, but he quickly waved me to silence. I nodded, and did as he wished, knowing full well his methods, and knowing he would bring me in on his thoughts when he could do so and felt it the right time. Now was obviously not the proper time. Instead Holmes continued to examine the contents of the home with his sharp eyes.

"Most impressive, Professor," Holmes stated in a friendly manner, as his eyes now fell upon the large clear crystal globe once again. "Rare crystal, is it not? And very old."

"Yes, ancient Egyptian, I believe, and of course, very old. Miranda can be most powerful at times—when she decides to give up her secrets. All my knowledge of other realms come to me through Miranda. In fact, I have been searching for a missing person myself, and I believe the cyclone has something to do with his disappearance. I have seen many strange things in the orb, however I can hardly make sense of their relevance. Let me see what my Miranda can show us of the whereabouts of this poor lost girl."

Professor Wonder slowly moved his hands over and around the large glass globe. Never did his hands actually touch it, but they came so close he was almost massaging it, and as he did so he spoke some arcane words I could not understand.

"More mumbo jumbo," I whispered to Holmes showing my exasperation at this entire farce. I was upset for I felt we were wasting our time here.

Sherlock Holmes smiled at me indulgently, "Not quite, Watson, actually it is ancient Sumerian."

"Right you are, Mr. Holmes," the Professor spoke up as he continued his mystical movements and arcane words.

I looked askance at my companion, "Sumerian?"

Holmes just gave me a slim grin.

"Let us see what Miranda can show us," the Professor continued softly.

"Miranda?" I asked curiously, for he had called the strange globe by that female name earlier and I was amused by it.

"Yes, it is the name I have given my magical crystal ball, Doctor," Professor Wonder explained to me simply. "Giving the crystal a name seems to bind the mystical connection between us more strongly. And of course, since she is female, I have given her a woman's name. Now, I will ask her your questions and we shall see what we shall see soon enough."

CHAPTER 5: WHAT MIRANDA TOLD US

"Miranda! Miranda! Come to me! Show me your visions of the whereabouts of young Dorothy Vale," Professor Wonder intoned, as he moved his hands mysteriously over the scintillating crystal of the glass-like globe. "I ask your help please, with all due diligence, to aid us in finding this poor lost child."

I was astonished by Wonder's actions and by his words spoken to the mysterious glass orb, as if he were actually talking to a real person—and as if he actually expected an answer. This time he spoke in English so I was able to understand him. However, I was more astonished by what happened next.

Professor Wonder gave me a sly wink, then explained to Holmes and myself, "It helps if I ask her nicely."

Holmes nodded, as if he was accepting of what I considered to be sheer farce. I could not imagine why Holmes gave this man such serious attention and latitude. I felt we should be gone from here straight away and spend our time in more worthy pursuits to find my missing niece. I found it difficult to hold myself in check regarding this foolishness.

"Hah, it just sounds like mere magical humbug!" I whispered to myself in a soft huff. Being the staunch man of science that I was, I could not help looking towards Holmes and wondering why he was tolerating this extraordinary nonsense. Even though Holmes had told me some of the Professor's words had been taken from the ancient Sumerian language, even I could see that it might have all been a part of his act. In fact, this entire situation seemed only worthy of some garish circus sideshow, or one of those spiritualist scams, such as those I had lately read about in the New York newspapers that the Magician Harry Houdini was debunking so effectively. I was sure that were the Great Houdini here to see this, he would uncover the sham right away. It made me wonder about Holmes. Nevertheless, I held my patience, and my tongue, for Holmes' benefit, for he seemed to think that there was some importance to what was to happen with this crystal ball, and as it turned out—he was entirely correct!

"Holmes?" I put the question to my friend softly.

"We will see, Watson. Please allow Professor Wonder to do his work in his own way and we shall see what he comes up with," my companion told me, rather patiently I thought, which was not often his way at all.

I just shook my head in growing despair, but held my patience in check for the moment, and for his sake.

The Professor moved his hands over the glowing orb most mysteriously. I had to admit, it appeared to be a most convincing act.

"I see it now. I see a vision forming through the clouded glass," the Professor spoke up all alert and eager. Then suddenly Holmes and I noticed the formerly clear glass had indeed clouded as if trying to form some vague image. It seemed amazing, incredible. A worthy trick, no doubt. I wondered how he did it. The three of us were all alert and looked intently into the cloudy globe as we saw that something was indeed forming there.

"By Jove!" I shouted in utter astonishment, in spite of my feelings on the matter.

A vision was indeed appearing now within the glass.

"Easy now, Watson," Holmes cautioned.

"Miranda, Miranda, let us see Dorothy Vale and what has become of her. Open the gate between these two worlds to your vision and show us what you see there, as you have shown these images to me in the past," Wonder intoned grandly, this time once again in English.

The cloudy globe slowly grew more clear to us. It was as if some portal had indeed opened and we were able to look inside to some other place or world and see some other images there—but what images!

It was the most bizarre thing that I had ever seen.

"Little men, Holmes! And are those wings? Blimey, they do have wings! No, they are not men, they are monkeys! By George, they appear to be winged monkeys! Have you ever seen such a thing!" I stammered, for such were the strange creatures I now saw before me clearly shown within the crystal globe that all three of us were astonished.

I looked upon the creatures closely with abject dread, for each one appeared most horrible. What did it all mean?

"Easy now, Watson," Holmes cautioned me once more. I could see he was no less intent upon what we were seeing before our eyes.

I was astonished and quickly blurted out, "Do you see it, Holmes!"

"I see it. Patience now, Watson, one thing at a time," my friend told me with a sharp knowing nod. Then he asked, "Professor Wonder, is your Miranda able to show you the girl yet?"

"No, but Miranda has never disappointed me. Dorothy Vale, come to me. Miranda, let me see her!"

Then I watched in astonishment as the close-up image of an old and angry looking woman's face filled the entire globe with her image—the woman's face was of a putrid aged pale skin color. The most incredible thing about her was that she had only one eye in the center of her head above her nose. Yet it was not any normal eye as we know it, that one eye was long and ghastly, for it seemed to have some expanding telescopic effect to it which was remarkable and at the same time most disturbing. That dread eye roved round and round out of it's socket to expand as if looking beyond…into some place else. A far seeing eye it surely was. It was very bizarre. Now we heard and saw all manner of sounds and images in the crystal orb. The old crone speaking, shouting loudly, a Lion roared in agony, there was a Scarecrow I could see in a field of some kind, and giant Sunflowers, then the old crone was heard shouting out harsh words or commands to the monkeys with wings!

Holmes suddenly spoke up, looking at me to say, "I have been taking note of a certain doctor, who has recently been elevated to the Professorship of a small Midlands university. He is now known as Professor Presbury. Have you heard of him? He would be most interested in these winged monkeys, no doubt."

"I can not say that I have," I replied matter-of-factly. "I can not recall any Presbury, either as a medical man, or a professor. No, I have not heard of him at all. What does he have to do with these monkeys that seem to have wings?"

"What indeed? Well, I am sure we shall hear of him some day. He is rumored to be experimenting with some mysterious elixir made of animal essence—whatever that might be?—which seems to cause the most incredible and extreme results, sometimes horribly violent."

"Well that sounds most disturbing."

"I have an inkling about this one, Watson. It seems that even the Scottish author, Robert Louis Stevenson got wind of this doctor's experiments years ago somehow and that he incorporated them into his now classic novel of fiction, *Dr. Jekyll and Mr. Hyde*. Or so it seems. I wonder about it."

It was all most strange for me to see this as I stared with rapt fascination into that crystal glass ball. It all seemed very much unearthly. Suddenly the old woman's words were now coming through more clearly to us, through Miranda, and now we were able to hear them perfectly.

"Now you shall suffer, as my slave!" the pale-skinned old hag spoke in an angry evil tone. She was a ghastly fiend.

"You're just an evil old witch!" a young girl's voice suddenly spoke out defiantly from nearby, and then we saw her! Dorothy Vale! My niece! She was there and alive!

Where ever *there* was?

"Holmes, it is her, my great niece, Dorothy! In the crystal globe!"

"Easy now, Watson, observe all most carefully," Holmes told me as he watched most intently.

The images flickered and changed, the perspective moved and blurred, and suddenly the one-eyed old crone's putrid face—Dorothy had called her a Witch—and she certainly looked like one to me—became more menacing. She was a terrible, scary sight to behold.

The old crone now threatened the young girl in a cold nasty voice, *"Come with me and see that you mind everything I tell you: for if you do not, I will make an end of you!"*

I was astonished to see and hear all this, it seemed truly impossible to me, but I was now convinced that it was not impossible at all. It was not some trick. How could it be? It had to be real! It seemed somehow to be too real—only too real! I feared greatly for my great niece now.

Take her away!" the old crone ordered in rage to two creatures who were obviously her henchmen, and we watched as they took the poor girl out of the room and away from Miranda's field of vision. Dorothy was soon gone.

Then the globe grew cloudy for another moment, and suddenly the Witch's evil face covered the globe and looked out at us directly, leering at us evilly with her wandering single eye. The eye telescoped as if to see us better. It was then plain to us that she could see us as clearly as we could see her through the crystal globe. It was uncanny and terrifying.

Then the vile old crone screamed out at us in rage, *"I see you! I know who you are! I was warned about you, Mr. Sherlock Holmes, and if you come here to Oz, know that I shall be waiting for you! You will find no victory here for you in Oz. This is my world, run by my rules, and you will be burned to cinders for your impudence and interference! Doom shall be your only result! Ah-ha-ha-ha-ha!"*

The one-eyed Witch continued to scream in delightful evil joy and then the crystal globe suddenly grew red hot.

"Did you hear it, Watson? She said 'Oz'!" Holmes told me curiously.

Then the crystal orb began to glow and turn red and heat up.

"Move back! Quickly!" the Professor warned sharply.

And then Miranda began to instantly exude great white smoke and glow red, soon to melt down before our eyes to quickly transform into a hot lump of useless molten slag. Miranda had now just become melted glass. How had this happened? It was sad and tragic. We were all shocked by this act, and how it had occurred so quickly. Sadly the Professor's crystal ball was now utterly destroyed. A small whiff of smoke rose up from the molten slag that was all that was left of the magic crystal glass that had once been Miranda.

"Poor creature! My Miranda is gone! That evil Witch killed her! She shall pay for that!" Professor Wonder promised us in hot anger, visibly enraged and utterly shocked by the loss of his beloved magical crystal. It was obvious he had some deeper relationship with Miranda than I could ever understand. He softly mumbled, "Miranda! Oh, my poor Miranda, I am so sorry!"

"I am heartily sorry about Miranda, Professor Wonder," Holmes said in a comforting voice. "Where did you ever obtain such a thing?"

"A long time ago. Actually I won it from an old Gypsy in a poker game. He was a bad man and told me he found it in the Rue Morgue in Paris, but that it would not work for him—but it did for me!" the Professor explained with a remembering sad smile.

"Most interesting, the Rue Morgue, you say?" Holmes replied with a nod of his head to me, and I could see his wonderful mind was working this information into his thoughts. I knew he was thinking of Mr. Poe's story. I wondered what it all might mean.

The Professor shook his head, then added sadly, "Nothing like that ever happened before when I called upon Miranda for her visions. In all the times I have gazed into the orb, never before has any apparition spoken to me! I never realized Miranda was a two-way means of vision and sound. This was not supposed to happen. That Witch must have some terrible power to do what she did to Miranda—doing it from her world—into our own! She will make a most dangerous foe to anyone who goes up against her. Your Dorothy is in great danger."

I looked at Holmes in surprise and shock as well. Had what we just witnessed with Miranda been real? Had it actually happened? Was Dorothy actually being held prisoner in some *outre* otherworldly land—the Witch had called it Oz—certainly an interesting sounding word. It was a word I had recently heard for the first time back in London. Holmes had mentioned the red poppy users as 'Opium Zombies' and the short word for them had become the acronym, 'OZ'. What did it all mean? Oz? Did such a place even exist? And if so, how in the silver blazes could Holmes and I ever find it, to rescue Dorothy from the Witch?

"Holmes?" I asked full of questions now, a bit unnerved by all I had just seen..

"Not now, Watson. I know you have a million questions but we must see if Professor Wonder here can find a way to transport us to this Oz place, to help save this poor girl who is in terrible danger," my companion told me in a deadly serious tone. I could see that he was well upon the case now, and I was thankful of the fact.

"Me?" said Professor Wonder. "How?"

Holmes smiled slightly, "Well, I have theories too, about these cyclones, and a particular friend's instructions call for self-propelling ones self into the eye of a cyclone at a precise moment, which can and will cause our desired effect!"

"Well, then, Mr. Holmes, I am sure that I can take us there. I have a hot-air balloon and it may prove just the trick to take us to Oz, but I will have to come with you to direct it into the center of the coming storm. We must act quickly, if you want the storm to take us to Oz— it has been a wish of mine to go there for quite a while, but frankly I was uncertain of success and hesitant to do it alone."

"Us?" I asked curiously nervous. "We are going to Oz? You are coming with us then? And what storm?"

"Yes, if you want to go to Oz to rescue Dorothy, I must come with you, and you two will be my crew. You will need me to pilot the balloon in any event," Wonder explained giving us each a most serious smile. He was not joking.

"And how do we do this?" I asked incredulous, with a nervous gulp.

The Professor looked at us and said seriously, "Simple really, we just use Mr. Holmes' calculations to hitch a ride on another storm, one of these Kansas cyclones, and it will take us. It may prove a difficult flight, but I think the three of us can handle my balloon. At least I hope so. Fortunately we are in Kansas and for our purposes there are very many of these gigantic storms almost every other day during this season. Another storm in this location should take us to the same location the previous storm took Dorothy. I have noticed they seem to move in patterns that can be predicted. Such is my theory, which I imagine we shall soon put to the test."

"Challenger has written of just such weather pattern theories," Holmes explained.

"Yes, yes, Professor Challenger! I have heard of him too!" Wonder stated most joyfully. "So he and I are in some agreement on this topic?"

"Yes, more than you might ever know," Holmes added with a nod of his regal head.

"Are you sure about this?" I asked Professor Wonder.

"Yes—well, mostly," he replied rather enigmatically. "I am now!"

"Then you are going to take us there?" Holmes asked Wonder showing his excitement.

"Certainly," the Professor replied, mirroring my friend's mood.

"That is grand, for we will need you and your advice once we arrive in Oz, Professor. So let us leave at once. I am most excited to be off! Are you ready, Watson?"

I looked over at my friend, the great detective Sherlock Holmes and nodded agreement, even though I was quite confused at the rapid turn events had lately taken. Things were moving so very fast. For instance, where were we actually going? To this nether realm of Oz? Really? Where was that located? And how would we get there? By hot-air balloon? It seemed improbable, even impossible.

"Let us be off immediately. Professor, please set out your balloon, I will start a fire in the brazier to heat the upper air in the bag, for if I am correct, by the look in the sky we are in the beginning stages of the creation of another massive cyclone storm."

"Right you are, Mr. Holmes. Come now, Doctor Watson, give me a hand with the pump of the balloon bag, and Mr. Holmes, you set the fire and stoke it brightly, then we shall soon be ready to take flight to Oz as soon as the storm appears and takes us."

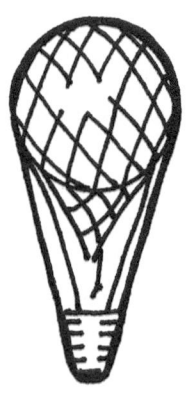

CHAPTER 6: A BALLOON RIDE TO OZ

Professor Wonder's Marvelous Magical Emporium Hot-Air Flying Balloon, as it was described in garish large colorful lettering upon the side, was soon ready, full of heated air and extended high into the sky. It had been filled with hot air from the furious fire that Holmes was tending most carefully in a small furnace in the basket below the overhead bag.

"Now we are ready to embark upon a great adventure," Professor Wonder stated showing his evident glee. I believe he was actually excited by going up high into the sky in such an untrustworthy device—during a terrible storm no less—and seeking to pilot his unwieldy craft into the very center of the turbulent and deadly singular eye of the cyclone. It was most incredible. It was quite unnerving for me, for I was a man who much preferred to have his feet firmly planted upon solid ground.

"You think it will be... reliable, Holmes?" I asked my friend, showing my doubts about the use of such a device for atmospheric travel. For 'reliable', I actually intended to use the word 'safe', but did not use that word in questioning my friend.

Holmes just nodded sagely, said with a smile, "Absolutely, Watson. It was Joseph and Jacques Montgolfier who made the first use of a hot air balloon in Paris in 1783, and it has proved a most viable mode of atmospheric travel since then. Did you know their first balloons were made out of paper?"

"Paper? Please tell me the Professor's balloon is *not* made of paper!"

Holmes gave me a rather indulgent smile, I knew he was humoring me, "Of course not, there have been significant improvements since then. Did you know that during the American Civil War such balloons were used on the battlefield for observation purposes? And as recently as 1870 during the Prussian siege of Paris, one hundred people and two million items of mail escaped in gas balloons!"

I did not know any of that, nor did I overly much care. I wondered where Holmes obtained his information, but I knew that he could be a fountain of knowledge if it had anything to do with a problem he had an interest in. However, his words of confidence did waylay some of my fear.

A new storm was certainly on the rise and coming our way, a large cyclone full of heavy rain and wild dangerous winds that blew in all directions, often simultaneously. It was a fury. Incredible winds as of hurricane force.

For his own part, Holmes smiled glibly and told me, "Fear not, Watson, this shall prove most interesting."

I certainly had my doubts. I gave my detective friend a sharp stare at his bold words. It was perhaps the understatement of the year, but I did not reply for at that moment Professor Wonder let go of all the guidelines that held down his balloon and we instantly shot upwards into the turbulent air—like one of Congreave's wartime rockets—right into the wild raging wind and rain at the center of the storm—and my stomach lurched right into my throat.

"Hold tight!" Professor Wonder warned us a bit after the fact, but Holmes and I needed no such warning as we both held on to the lines on the rim of the basket for dear life. It was a close run thing that at any moment, any one of our intrepid trio—or all three of us—might be plucked out of that basket and sent down to our doom to who knows where. But we held on. We held on for dear life.

Our balloon was instantly sucked into the vortex of the mighty storm. Upwards and upwards the balloon took us, our small basket buffeted by the mighty winds and driving rain. It was a torrential turbulence. The three of us were soon soaked through and through. Seeing the raging cyclone from the inside was an incredible experience certainly, but one I was not overly fond of. Holmes, however, seemed to be enjoying it quite a bit, even going so far as to making various comments about the power of the storm and other aspects of it with the Professor. They spoke of air speed and wind direction as if in an Oxford classroom. Holmes even brought up some theories from Challenger's book that he said now were proved to be correct. I am sure Challenger would be most pleased to hear that news. I could only hunker down in sheer terror. Most of my thoughts had to do with the incredible danger we were in if anything went wrong. To say I was not amused, was a vast understatement. Holmes, however, seemed as happy as a youth riding his first circus carousel. I could not fathom it.

Professor Wonder did seem to know his business and controlled our tiny craft rather well, continually moving various levers and opening and closing valves that seemed to control his balloon and allow it to move in a certain direction.

"We are on course, Mr. Holmes!" The Professor stated jubilantly.

"Yes, I have connected Challenger's theories with your own on cyclones and we have come up with a working plan to travel through the cyclone. We are on course, as I predicted," Holmes stated confidently.

Hearing that did much to ally my fears. It was obvious our balloon was moving in the direction Holmes had in mind. Or so I hoped. I wondered where he was taking us. I knew it was to Oz—but where was that?

The Professor at times dropped heavy sandbags and worked rudders on the basket and constantly manipulated long levers to control our flight. Holmes and I helped him under his guidance to send our balloon in what I could tell now was a very specific direction that he wanted us to go. Finally we came through a particularly thick wall of rain and wind to find ourselves in a rather calm and less windy area. The rain had almost stopped entirely. It was most uncanny, for I knew we were still inside the cyclone—in fact, we were within the very center of it!

"We have reached our goal, gentlemen, the center of the storm, the eye of the beast as it were," Professor Wonder told us triumphantly. "The turbulence will abate here for a time. We can relax a bit now and allow our balloon to move with the storm. I am sure now that we are within the storm's center—the exact area where the Vale home with Dorothy in it must have been transported—and even though this is a different storm—it should take us directly to the same location where Dorothy was taken. Or such is my theory."

"This Oz place?" I asked curiously, the tone in my voice showing that I was doubting that it even existed.

"Yes, Oz!" the Professor shouted triumphantly, "it does exist and we are on the way to it, doctor!"

I could only look at Holmes in a most curious manner.

"I hope you remembered to bring your revolver, Watson," Holmes asked me in a rather confidential tone.

I looked at him carefully and just nodded, patting the cold metal gun that was secure in my coat pocket. I was soaking wet, as were we all from the wild wind and pelting rain, but feeling the hard steel of my revolver in my hand gave me some security and comfort, for who knew what we would find in this strange land of Oz? Witches? Terrible monkeys with wings? What else could there be, I wondered?

"We are on the way!" the Professor repeated in utter delight, in a tone that never doubted we were truly moving towards our destination.

"Yes, indeed!" Sherlock Holmes agreed in an excited tone now, but I could see he was waiting. Patient. He could be most patient at times when there was something he was intensely interested in. He was calm as all get-out, seemingly thinking about what was to come, and making his plans to deal with it. Oh, how I envied him!

I on the other hand, was a bundle of raw nerves and barely repressed terrors. I will not recount to you the dire thoughts and fearful trepidations that were swirling within my mind as we rode through the outer wall of that turbulent storm. The whipping rain and wind was terrible. It seemed even more powerful than the wall of wind and rain we had first passed through. It was the most amazing thing I had ever done in my life—it even made my war service in Afghanistan pale by comparison.

The winds of the cyclone had taken us far and wide now. After many hours I noticed that we had even been lifted far over a magnificent gloriously colorful rainbow. It was a lovely sight that shone bright in the dazzling sunlight.

"There is your rainbow, Watson!" Holmes stated with a wry grin,

"Yes, is it not beautiful?"

Then the Professor reset the controls as Holmes requested and we suddenly did a gradual descent and soon landed rather calmly upon the ground. It was certainly good to be back on solid and dry *terra firma* again—but as I looked around me I noticed that this was ground unlike anything I had ever seen before.

CHAPTER 7: HOLMES
AND WATSON IN OZ

"I say, Holmes, this is most certainly not Kansas!" I spoke these words with the utmost astonishment for my eyes were amazed by what I beheld. It was one of the most strange and alien landscapes I had ever imagined and it stretched far away to the horizon. Even my service in the wild lands of Afghanistan, nor my readings of the fantastic scientific novels of Mr. Wells and Mr. Verne could not compare with this amazing sight. Sherlock Holmes gave me a wan smile, "Right you are, Watson!"

"We have arrived, gentlemen. I present to you, the Wonderful Land of Oz!" Professor Wonder told us beaming with joyful excitement, as he worked to stabilize his descending hot-air balloon. He tethered the lines firmly to make sure our traveling conveyance was now held secure on the ground, and us with it. "It is just as Miranda showed it to me!"

Holmes quickly put out the fire in the small furnace above our basket that heated the air of the balloon. We did not need it any longer. We had finally touched down on the ground, for which I was most grateful. Now I could look at the vast landscape around me in closer examination and I found myself viewing it in utter amazement. I could see that my two companions felt the same way by the astonished looks upon their faces. What I saw was a land of marvelous beauty with patches of green and gorgeous flowers, birds with brilliant plumage, a strange but beautiful sight.

The three of us were utterly gobsmacked by what we saw. It was not like anything we had ever seen before.

We found that our balloon had actually come down in the center of a park of some kind, or a field of what was apparently a deserted small city or village. But what a village it was! It was not small in the sense of length or breadth, but in the sense that it was apparently a village for very small people. Tiny-sized people. The buildings were also small in size, built of a riot of bright round shapes with all types of roof designs, all of which were blue. So it appeared blue was the favorite color here. I wondered why? I had never seen the likes of any of this before.

"Amazing, Watson!" was all Holmes said. "Simply amazing!"

"Yes, but what is it?"

"Why, it is Oz, Doctor!" the Professor responded gleefully.

But what was this 'Oz'? I thought.

That was the question we would now seek to answer.

My companions and myself saw no inhabitants of this tiny person village to prove to us any little people actually lived here now, nor did anyone come out to greet us. They were surely small in size. Were they some type of leprechaun? Who could tell. We looked around us for some hint of what the people who lived here might look like. Everything was very quite, a very pregnant silence hung over the place, as if waiting for something, or someone.

Holmes and I, with Professor Wonder had stepped out of the balloon basket and after I helped them to tether the landing lines to nearby trees, we walked around a bit. Exploring. We saw trees that were quite amazing, being of extraordinary sizes, shapes and colors. Nothing like this existed back home at all. These were brightly hued trees and also plants of all types that surrounded us with large leafy fronds that scintillated in the bright sun light which shone down upon us from high overhead. Some of the leaves of these plants seemed to make wonderful chime sounds. Others glowed brightly and shined. It was quite extraordinary. As I looked around me further, I saw that the entire village was comprised of brightly colored tiny houses surrounded by gaily hued plants and trees that shone with vibrant colors, some sporting hues that I was certain I had never seen before as any Earthly colors.

"My Lord, Holmes! I have never seen anything like this in my life," I muttered to my detective friend who was looking around him almost as amazed as I was. He seemed to be taking note of everything, taking it all in like some great sponge, into his magnificent vault of a mind. I wondered what he made of it all. He was certainly interested—interested beyond all measure.

"Quite fascinating, Watson," Holmes told me in what I took to be a very understated tone. "In fact, I find this all exquisitely fascinating."

I could not disagree with him.

"The Land of Oz!" Professor Wonder announced with pride and an expansive waving of his arms, once again offering us a sly wink as though he was more familiar with the place than we were.

Then Wonder went on to explain further, "I have seen many images of this very village through my crystal ball, Miranda, poor thing. I never dreamed it was real! That Witch will pay for what she did to my crystal. Miranda showed me many wonders here in Oz, but I only dared to actually travel here in the flesh to witness them for myself with you two to come with me. Look at the vibrant colors and the wonderful landscape. Truly lovely and amazing. You see nothing like this back home."

"Nor in London," I stated in an awed whisper.

"Nor upon the world of Earth that we are familiar with," Holmes added thoughtfully, with a sage nod of his aquiline head.

I took my companion's words to heart for as I continued to look around me I could see an entire village—a most alien place that appeared to be deserted—a village of little people certainly—but where were the people? There were no inhabitants in evidence yet, no one had come out to meet us, but I had the uncanny feeling that the miniscule inhabitants of this strange place must be hiding from us, safe away in their tiny cottages, or hunkered down behind the bushy trees or tall grass and leafy flowers. They were there, I was sure of it, but they were not coming out to greet us. Not yet. I wondered why. I felt they were watching us closely. I put this to Holmes.

"Yes, Watson, I suspect the inhabitants are nearby, certainly watching us most closely, most carefully, perhaps too fearful to show themselves to us at the moment."

"What could put such fear into them?" I asked sharply, but then I recalled that old terrifying one-eyed Witch I had seen in Wonder's crystal ball Miranda, and I did not need to be told why anyone might be fearful. Just recalling that terrible image of the Witch's face, and her monstrous Cyclops single eye, put a shiver of fear into me I shall never forget.

"What indeed?" Holmes replied in his usual enigmatic style. I could not tell what he was thinking, but his fine mind was surely working overtime as he noted our surroundings most carefully.

"Yes, Mr. Holmes, Doctor, these are little people, gentle folk, they know none of the baser feelings many of our own larger folk know only too well. These little people are gentle and fun loving—but fearful," the Professor explained carefully. Then he added, "Or so I have seen through my Miranda."

"How so? What exactly have you seen about this place?" I asked, curious at just how much the Professor knew about this enigmatic land of Oz. For I was now certain he knew far more than he was telling us.

"I have been watching this place for a time and I have seen terror running loose in this land, Doctor," the Professor stated in a grim whisper. "Terrible evil lurks abroad and the little people here, and inhabitants in other places in Oz, are terrified."

I nodded, I could well understand that, for had Miranda not shown us images of the dread winged monkeys, and the putrid pale-faced one-eyed wicked crone who was called the Witch of the West? But I wondered why these little people should fear us, and why hide from us? We certainly wished them no harm. Little did I realize that I would soon receive an explanation for that situation, and much more.

"They are certainly lurking about, but hiding," Holmes told us carefully. "I can hear them there—there—and there! I know where they are but I do not want to startle them by confronting them before they are ready. They are small people, and are rather shy, and fearful of strangers, and with good reason."

"So what should we do?" I asked impatient to get to the nub of the matter here, and then be on our way to find Dorothy.

"Do?" Holmes stated with a smile. "Well, I imagine we should be proper English gentlemen and introduce ourselves."

I nodded my agreement, it seemed the proper thing to do, after all.

That said, my companion stood forward from us and spoke up in a firm calm voice, "Hello, all! I am Sherlock Holmes of London, and these are my companions, Doctor John Watson, and Professor Wonder who is from Kansas. We have come here to visit your lovely land to locate the missing girl-child named Dorothy. Have you seen her, or heard of her?"

There was no sound, no word came to us in reply for a long moment. Then from out of their places of hiding we heard the questions muttered among them, "Dorothy?"

"They are seeking Dorothy?"

"Then you are friends of Dorothy?" Someone asked us.

"Yes, of course, we are friends of Dorothy," I explained in a loud tone for all to hear. "In fact, I am her great uncle John Watson, come here to rescue her."

"Dorothy!" a high voice muttered, that was followed by a chorus of rather high-pitched girlish type laughter.

"Yes, Dorothy!" a deeper voice repeated.

"A friend of Dorothy, he says!" another voice spoke up in a tone of joy with more light giggles of laughter.

"Yes, Dorothy!" I told them all a bit impatiently. I could not see what was so funny. "Of course!"

Then the queerest people I had ever seen outside of a circus came out from hiding and showed themselves. The little people of the village were soon in full view to us. They were an odd and very unusual group, but a colorful and seemingly joyful lot of small-sized folk with smiling faces.

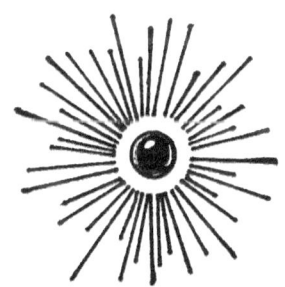

CHAPTER 8: HOLMES AND WATSON IN MUNCHKINLAND

As if on cue, hundreds of very small people came out to joyfully greet us. They were the queerest people as I have said, small and oddly dressed, with all manner of colorful hats that rose to a point a foot over their heads! The men were all dressed in blue with incredibly shiny boots with coils on the top. The men were also dressed all the same, but the overall appearance was of wee size people that would have found a better home at a carnival or a circus. Both men and women wore tiny black pearls that hung from the brim of their pointed hats. The pearls tinkled as they moved. It was most strange. I had never seen a black pearl—but they seemed to be quite normal here. In fact, the entire village, and the people who lived here, seemed to have come full blown from some incredible otherworldly circus—in this strange carnival-looking world. It was all very much incredible to see.

The little people carefully approached Holmes, Professor Wonder and myself. They came closer, very curious, with laughter of joy and happiness. They prodded us and touched our clothing, which they seemed to think was quite funny or strange. I did not have the heart to tell them that we felt the same way about them. They seemed to be a most gentle and lovely little folk, child-like in many ways—though most were obviously fully adult, while there were also children among them that were even smaller than the adults, and yet there was something strangely familiar about them. The men sported all manner of fancy facial hair—vast whiskers, bushy beards and lush mustachios that were long and groomed wondrously. I could barely fathom it. Or them.

They looked closely at us, and we looked closely at them in awe.

"Holmes," I whispered to my detective companion, "do they not remind you in some way of... Tonga?"

"Yes, they do, Watson," Holmes replied in a low whisper, "but we shall keep that bit of news mum for now, until we learn more."

I nodded, I was relieved that it appeared Holmes believed there might be some connection between that little beast Tonga, and these little folk—though what it could be alluded me. The difference could not be more stark, and yet, as I recalled the evil little fellow, I could see he might have sprung from these very people.

Finally, a rather well-fed one of these small folk came boldly towards us out from his fellows and spoke up in a powerful voice, "Welcome! Welcome dear friends of Dorothy the Witch-killer, welcome to Munchkinland!"

"Hello! Dorothy the Witch-killer? Munchkinland? What are Munchkins?" Holmes asked thoughtfully.

"Munchkinland?" I said softly. What a strange name. I assumed then that these were the Munchkinland people—or Munchkins? Indeed, I would soon learn that was their name.

"Yes, we are Munchkins," the small man told us simply with a winning smile. He was dressed fully in blue clothing, as were all the other men here.

"So you are Munchkins? Then you are not leprechauns?" I asked, showing my incredulity.

They all shook their heads, "We have never heard of any leprechauns. Where do they live? We are Munchkins, and this is our land."

"In the Magical Land of Oz," the Munchkin told us further, obviously, he was some type of leader here.

"'Oz' again!" Holmes said softly, thoughtfully. "This is the second time we have come across that odd word—in London and now here. Although what it might mean I do not know yet."

I nodded, not knowing what to make of all this. I looked towards Holmes and whispered, "They are a rather charming looking little people."

Holmes just smiled indulgently at my words, then looked towards the little man dressed in blue, "Can you help us find Dorothy?"

"Find Dorothy?" he asked seriously.

"He wants to find Dorothy," another of the miniscule folk repeated.

"Yes, we need to find Dorothy," I stated seriously, for I wanted to impress upon all of them the importance of our mission. "She is in danger and needs our help."

"Well then, you must go to The City of Emeralds, there is no other way, absolutely no other way to go about it," another Munchkin explained.

"And why is that? Is that where the Witch of the West has her castle?" I asked, for I knew my niece was being held captive in the Witch's castle. Holmes and I had seen as much through Miranda. I did not want to make a side trip to any City of Emeralds, if I did not have to do so. I was sure that Holmes felt the same way as I did about that, but he was characteristically remaining silent just then, for some reason I could not determine.

The Munchkins all drew back a step at my words. Obviously the Witch was not popular here at all. I could easily understand why, but I had no knowledge of just how wicked that Witch could be, and had been, to these small peaceful people.

"They want to find the sorceress Dorothy," one of the small people whispered to those around him.

"Dorothy is in danger!" another of the wee folk whispered back.

"Why?" asked another curiously.

These little people seemed to be a rather curious bunch.

I explained simply, "Why, we are here to save her, of course, and to bring her safely back to her home in Kansas."

They all seemed to consider that most carefully, talking among themselves for a moment, then they seemed to come to some decision.

"Then you surely must seek out the Wizard," the little man told us in a firm tone.

"The Wizard?" I asked.

"Who is this Wizard?" Holmes asked, showing a marked interest now.

"He is Oz. Dorothy was here, and we sent her to see him, for no one else in Oz could help her. She told us she landed here from a place called Kansas, which was the home of her civilized country, and the Wizard is going to tell her how to get back home," the man told us in a serious tone. "Oz is the only one who can work such magical wonders."

Holmes looked up, "And where may we find this Oz?" "Why, in The City of Emeralds, of course," another Munchkin told us.

All the Munchkins nodded their heads in serious agreement.

By now we were surrounded by a multitude of these little folk. They were touching us curiously, but being most friendly. Now that they knew we were no threat, and knowing we were friends of Dorothy, they were busy greeting us and introducing themselves to us as well.

For the most part, almost all the Munchkins who introduced themselves and their family members to us had rather strange, difficult to pronounce names that were most confusing to me. However, they were all the most friendly little people I had ever met. But Holmes and I had scant time for making acquaintances and forging new friendships, for we needed to find Dorothy as soon as possible.

"I am sure, Watson, that Dorothy is in the most extreme danger at the hands of this Witch of the West. Not immediately, however, so we do have some time, for I could tell through Miranda that the wicked woman relishes the fact of holding Dorothy as a captive and slave, and keeping the girl in her power for some reason. I have dealt with this type of criminal mind before and can tell you that this evil woman is scheming to find some way to punish Dorothy that would be in the most heinous manner she can devise. However, I also believe that the woman has some other motive for not harming Dorothy immediately, but as yet, I can not discern what that might be."

The first Munchkin we had met had heard Holmes words, and spoke up, "Right you are! The Witch is seeking her revenge and it is sure to be most terrible. You see, it was Dorothy who dropped that house on the Witch's wicked sister, the Witch of the East, killing her dead. Dorothy also now wears the Witch's silver shoes, they hold some mysterious power, and the Witch of the West coverts them most intently."

"How do you know this?" Holmes asked the little fellow.

"We were there when it happened. We saw it, and over there is her house," he replied simply pointing beyond the trees.

I saw Holmes nod his head at this news. I wondered what it might mean, but by the look upon his face, I could see it seemed to answer one of his questions.

"So that first Witch is now dead?" I asked our little friends. "That would be The Witch of the East?"

"Most assuredly, that is her, and she is most definitely dead!" the Munchkins added in a chorus of cheers.

I looked over to where the Munchkins were pointing now and saw what had to be Uncle Henry and Aunt Em's farmhouse blown here from faraway Kansas. It had somehow been transported here to Oz, and in perfect condition, much as we had been transported here, though we came in the Professor's hot-air balloon, not in a Kansas farmhouse through a cyclone as had Dorothy

"Most interesting," Holmes spoke up softly as he carefully looked over at the house. The fact that it was in near perfect condition, apparently undamaged by the vast travel through the cyclone seemed incredible. "Once again, Challenger's theories on these phenomena prove to be correct."

"How so, Holmes?" I asked eager to hear some explanation of these strange events.

"Later, Watson…" my companion replied to me in a whisper.

"Well, it is definitely Dorothy's home from Kansas," I said in surprise. "However did it get here?"

"Through the storm," Holmes told me simply.

"And not receive any damage from that wild flight through the sky?"

Sherlock Holmes just nodded, and I knew he was referring me once more to the theories of Professor Challenger upon these severe storms that can be both fierce and gentle at the same time—so totally arbitrary. Just one of the wonders of this strange land.

The Professor just shook his head in dismay, "All the way from Kansas, it is truly remarkable how it traveled all the way here to Oz. I always thought so, but never really believed!"

"It is absolutely incredible!" I stammered in awe.

"Not so incredible, as we have proved with the Professor's balloon," Holmes reminded us.

"And under that house was found the dead body of the Witch of the East," Professor Wonder told us. "Only her legs, feet, and her silver shoes were visible from under the house. The rest of the home covered her body. I saw the image through Miranda days ago, but did not know what it meant until now."

"So the farm house went through the storm, with Dorothy inside it, and arrived here of all places. I find it beyond incredible that a Kansas farmhouse could be transported here undamaged," I said unable to hold back my amazement.

Holmes smiled and told me, "How, indeed, Watson? I am sure that we shall encounter many magical and mysterious events in this land of Oz—do you not feel it? The presence of something…else…something almost super natural in origin."

"It is magic, Mr. Holmes. I for one feel it too, most certainly," the Professor told us.

The Munchkins surrounding us listening to our words just laughed and giggled in obvious delight. They knew, far better than us, that Oz was a most magical place.

CHAPTER 9: THE GOOD WITCH OF THE NORTH

Suddenly there appeared a white-gowned older woman who came towards us with a glowing smile that was like pure sunshine. She said quite simply, "Hello! I am the Witch of the North."

"You are a Witch?" I asked her showing my evident surprise.

"Of course," she replied with a lilting laugh that was full of joy. Her happiness and positive attitude seemed most infectious and made her seem younger than she actually was.

"But I thought Witches were putrid like that one with the one eye?" I asked, quite confused by all this magical mayhem.

Holmes only smiled, but said nothing when I looked to him for guidance.

"Only evil Witches are ugly. I am The Good Witch of the North of Oz, and these little ones, the Munchkins are my friends. I look after them as much as I am able. Now the question is, who are you?" she asked still friendly, but suddenly grown serious.

"I am Sherlock Holmes, and this is Doctor John Watson," my detective companion offered, and I could see he was most struck by the majesty of this most unique mature woman. I saw in Holmes the same admiration in his eyes for her that I had seen him often show when talking about that other wondrous female he only spoke of as 'The Woman'—the amazing Irene Adler. It was most interesting for me to see this sudden admiration from my friend towards a person of the opposite sex after so long a time. It had been many years since Holmes had seen Irene Adler, but I knew he thought of her often.

"And I am Professor Wonder, master of exotica and all manner of arcane knowledge, among other marvelous and sundry things."

"What are you doing here and how may I help you?" the woman asked continuing her friendly tone and manner.

"We came here—from another place—to rescue Dorothy. We have discovered she is being held prisoner in a castle by the Witch of the West. Can you help us free Dorothy?" Holmes asked thoughtfully. He looked the woman over most carefully, and evidently liked what he saw.

The Witch of the North simply smiled, "Dorothy? Dorothy from Kansas? Well she is quite a bold girl, quite the hero hereabouts. If Dorothy is indeed held captive by the evil Witch she is in grave danger. The Witch has a large secure castle and an army of slave soldiers and winged monkeys—among other creatures that do her bidding—so she is quite invulnerable to any attack."

"Nevertheless we must rescue Dorothy," I spoke up.

"Yes, Doctor Watson is quite right. He is Dorothy's great uncle. He and I have traveled a long distance to secure Dorothy's release so we could bring her back home to her family," Holmes explained with his usual resolve.

"And I brought them here in my hot air balloon so we could save the poor girl," the Professor added.

Holmes nodded, then asked the Good Witch, "Can you help us?"

"Well, you must seek out the Wizard for something that involves that kind of complicated magic against such a powerful Witch," the woman informed us with equal resolve.

"The Wizard!" a Munchkin voice repeated from his place of hiding.

"The Wizard of Oz!" another of the wee folk spoke in a whisper, and I could not help but think of them as some form of leprechaun—and now the sudden realization came to me that Tonga—from our own world—must surely have been one of them as well.

I asked Holmes about this but he said not a word.

It was the Good Witch who hearing my query answered it with the most astonishing news I had yet heard in Oz, "You are correct, Doctor. There once were two Munchkin brothers, long ago, Tonga and Songa, but their souls became evil and twisted. They were banished by the Munchkins for their use of the red poppy, they made a powerful powder out of it that enslaved them to it, and so they became acolytes of the Witch of The West and did her bidding. However, I have not heard their names spoken in many years."

I looked to Holmes and he motioned for me to remain silent. I did not say that I had been the one to kill Tonga many years ago, but the fact that he had an evil brother still alive sent my nerves to quivering. I had never thought of this possibility.

I looked at the Munchkins with a new realization and wondered just what Holmes would think of my thoughts. I was sure he was far ahead of me on this tack, and in fact, it may have been one reason why he had accompanied me on my trip to America in the first place, which began this entire adventure in Oz.

There was much to think about with this new information about Tonga and Songa, as the Munchkins were busy talking among themselves.

We heard yet a third hidden Munchkin whisper, "You must go and see the Wonderful Wizard of Oz."

The Witch of the North laughed delightfully. "My little Munchkin friends. They are fearful of the Witch, and with good reason. As I told you, she has even caused some of their kind to turn bad—to serve her. These have been banished, but enough of that for now."

I looked to Holmes and saw that his attention had perked up considerably, but he did not ask the Good Witch for any further explanation. I wondered if he already knew as much, but had just had his theories corroborated?

"Thank you and the Munchkins for directing us to the Wizard and for your information on the Witch—it shall be of use if we ever encounter her," Holmes replied to her with a sure nod of his head.

"She is a most foul creature. Her magical powers are diminished when she is far from her home. The problem for you—and Dorothy—is that you must go into the Witch's domain to rescue Dorothy. That is where the evil Witch has her castle and where she is most powerful. But first you must go to the City of Emeralds to see Oz, The Great and Terrible. Only a Wizard can help you now with such a complicated problem," the Witch of the North told us in warning.

I saw Holmes slowly nod his head in acknowledgement.

"The Land of Oz is a wondrous place, and you are all welcome to stay here with us if you like," one of the little women told us with a most welcoming grin. "Or if you like, we will help you to travel to The City of Emeralds to see the Wizard. Your choice. The Wizard will be able to answer all your questions and help you to defeat the wicked Witch and save Dorothy."

Holmes nodded, "Very well, then we shall be off to the City of Emeralds immediately."

"How do we get there?" I asked the Witch of the North.

"My best advice for you is to follow yonder road made of yellow bricks, Mr. Holmes, Doctor Watson, and you, Professor Wonder," the Witch told us with a delightful smile I shall never forget, "it shall lead you to the city of the Great and Terrible Oz."

So we did as the Good Witch told us to do. Holmes and I, with Professor Wonder, began to take our leave of Munchkinland, walking away from the village, onto the road made of bright yellow bricks to follow it wherever it led us. The Munchkins waved us goodbye and cheered us upon our quest.

Some of the younger Munchkins, smaller in size—I assumed they were children—followed Holmes out of the village as if he were the pied piper. For some reason they were drawn to him. One of them spoke up saying how they would do whatever they could to help us in our quest for Dorothy. Their leader, a spry and sharp one by the strange name of Boq—who reminded me somewhat of Wiggins—told us he and his fellows would be ever alert to help us in any way they were able. I was enchanted by them all, as I am sure, was Holmes.

"I thank you all, and I appreciate your keeping your eyes open about the actions of the wicked Witch," Holmes told the young Munchkins as he smiled at them and their leader.

"Amazing wee folk, eh Holmes?"

"Yes, Watson, and perhaps they will form a new Oz contingent of my Irregulars here in Munchkinland?"

"Indeed!" I replied with a grin as we continued our journey. The Witch of the North told us to keep an eagle eye out for danger, for she assured us that danger lurked everywhere in Oz and that the Witch of the West was a most formidable enemy. I ensured her that we would be most wary, and be on our guard at all times.

"Beware the minions of the Witch of the West, as well, she has various servants and slaves, each one more vile than the next," the Good Witch alerted us as she blew each one of us a delightful goodbye kiss.

Then we were on our way, traveling down the road of yellow bricks, out of Munchkinland and into the countryside of Oz, on our way towards the City of Emeralds, as the Good Witch and all the charming wee Munchkins waved us a fond farewell.

CHAPTER 10: ALONG THE ROAD OF YELLOW BRICKS

The three of us walked for many hours, much of it without any conversation, as we each communed internally, our minds thinking over our own personal thoughts. I, for one, had much to think about. I had seen many strange things since I had come to this land of Oz, much that was simply inexplicable to me. Was it just a coincidence that this land—Oz—and the problem back in London of the 'OZ' Opium Zombies—were the same word? Was there some connection? I was sure that Holmes thought there was. Little did I realize that it was just the beginning of the wonders, and the horrors, that were in store for us.

Holmes and I, along with Professor Wonder, knew that we were on the most amazing journey, and what would be the most utterly fantastic adventure of our very lives. I told this to Holmes and he just shuffled it off a bit as if the fact did not impress him greatly. I knew then that he had something else upon his mind. I could see that it was weighing heavily upon him.

"What is it, Holmes? Won't you tell me?" I asked my friend when I felt the opportunity to question him presented itself. We were walking on the yellow road which now ran through a very pastoral countryside. So far, this was a rather pleasant land to travel through. It reminded me somewhat of the lovely gardens of Kent in our own land of south England. If this was the dangerous land that the Witch of the North spoke of for us in Oz, then it seemed to me that there would be very little danger at all. At least for the present. We continued walking upon the ever-winding road made of yellow bricks.

I looked at my companion, waiting for his answer to my question about what was troubling him. He saw my look, knew I was expectant of an answer from him. I waited for his reply patiently.

Holmes looked grim, finally he told me, "I see I cannot put you off any longer. So be it! Just know that all is not as it seems here, Watson."

"Well, indeed, I certainly agree with you there! For this very day I have seen faraway lands, strange people and—Witches—both good and bad ones. Who would have believed that any of this was possible? Or even real?" I said, not hiding my amazement and puzzlement at it all.

"Yes, that is true, and that is all well and good."

"Then there is something more? What is it that bothers you so, Holmes?" I continued to prod him for a reply. I could always tell when he was in a bothersome mood.

Sherlock Holmes looked at me closely, "Watson, did you not remember what that old crone of a wicked Witch told me before she destroyed Miranda?"

"I... Well... I am sorry, no Holmes, but I am afraid I do not recall exactly—so much was going on at the time, you know."

"Yes, of course, I almost missed her words myself, so unexpected was it to hear what she said in all the confusing phantasmagoria of that Witch's threats and her impending attack upon Miranda—but do you not recall that the Witch had not only recognized my name—she said she had been *warned* of my coming."

I looked at Holmes incredulous, "But that is not possible!"

"I know."

"But who could possibly warn her?" I asked in utter surprise.

"Who indeed?" he responded in a low thoughtful tone.

"It is not possible," I stated with a certainty. "How could she possibly be warned of your coming here to Oz?"

"That is what I thought as well, but it seems that it is *not* impossible. We are here in this world far from our own—and we have already seen in the Professor's crystal ball—through poor Miranda—that there exists a device which can communicate between our own world, and this one. It appears that there may be others who also have similar devices. Perhaps that wicked Witch herself may have some type of crystal ball that she can use to communicate to someone else... between the worlds? Between this world and our own. My thoughts race at the implications, and the dangers, that somehow that Witch is communicating with someone in our own world. And I fear who that someone might be."

"Holmes?" I asked him gravely, my concern growing now at what this might mean. "It simply cannot be."

My companion continued carefully, "Tonga, Songa, Dorothy and us, who knows how many others have crossed between our worlds? I do not pretend to know how these crystal globes work, but that they do work, is incontrovertible. One of these devices is most certainly in the possession of that vile Witch—but I believe there may be other individuals who also have possession of one of these crystal devices. I fear who would have the one that is located in our home world?"

"Well, Professor Wonder had one in our world! Miranda," I answered him.

"Yes, and it appears there may be others, or at least one other, as well."

I nodded gravely, "I suppose that makes sense."

"You know that it does. There is a definite connection between our worlds. How, exactly, I do not know for certain."

I looked aghast at Holmes, for I could see that he was most seriously concerned upon the matter. That realization did little to bolster my own spirits. I wondered just what he meant, what was in his darkest thoughts, but Holmes would say no more upon the subject. He was like that at times, not divulging his thoughts until he had solid evidence to build a theory or to take a course of action. I just had to accept this information for now and it did not bolster my spirits.

We continued walking onwards down the road, and soon my attention was attracted when I heard Professor Wonder suddenly call from ahead of us where he was leading our intrepid trio along the road through Oz. He verbally prodded us, "Come along now, gentlemen, do not dilly-dally. It would not be wise for you to lag behind and for us to become separated."

"Right you are, Professor," I told him, so Holmes and I quickened our pace to catch up with him. Soon all three of us were walking briskly side-by-side along the brick road.

I spoke no more with Holmes of his discovery about the wicked Witch having been warned about him, by name. How could such a thing be possible? The more I thought about it, the more I realized there was a deeper aspect to this strange world of Oz than met the eye.

Our intrepid trio continued our trek upon the cobblestones of the yellow road, and as we did so we looked all around us and took in the brightly colored flowers and fauna that seemed to predominant in this wonderful land of Oz. It was a most exquisite and lovely sight, a quite intoxicating land run riot with bright colors and scintillating light. Holmes had taken it in, as well as a few samples for testing. I had never seen anything like it before in my life. It was truly a magical place, but I knew only too well that there was a dark side to that magic.

We continued our trek along the road of yellow bricks for the next few hours. We were getting tired and hungry. We had been walking all day.

"Mr. Holmes, I am glad your young Munchkin irregulars prepared us these small bags of food and victuals to eat and drink for our long journey," Professor Wonder stated as we came to a crossroads.

"Yes, and they may prove to be more useful to us yet," Holmes replied. Then with a slim smile he added, "I have taken some time with Boq and his young friends, and they are quite inquisitive and innovative fellows. They seem to miss nothing, and they will help us best they can. I shall not dissuade them."

"Where to now?" I asked my companion, seeing another road that cut across the yellow bricked one and wondering where it might lead.

"We must stay on this road, upon the yellow bricks, gentlemen," the Professor told us most definitely. "Such was the Good Witch's advice, and I would not go against it."

I nodded, and Holmes and I followed the Professor across the intersecting black road to continue along the yellow road. We walked onward and came to a more dense part of the woods on either side of the road.

"Holmes, Professor, there seem to be some rather large tree branches and limbs that have fallen onto the road up ahead, so watch your step," I warned my companions as we neared a thick part of the woods where large leafy trees had overgrown very close to the edge of both sides of the road.

"Ah, yes, Watson, I see them," Holmes told us as he walked closer to the rather thick fallen branches that lay upon the road, almost blocking it. He stopped and immediately examined them most carefully.

"What is it, Holmes?" I asked concerned now.

Suddenly my friend nodded, and spoke up in a sharp tone, "Just as I thought."

"Whatever do you mean, Mr. Holmes?" the Professor asked curious now.

I echoed the question, now looking directly at Holmes.

The Great Detective nodded slightly, "They have definitely been this way. See this sharp cut to each of these branches and the tree limbs. They have all been cut by a very large and sharp object."

"A knife," the Professor asked quickly.

"Perhaps a sword?" I added, my previous military life coming to the fore.

Holmes merely smiled indulgently at us, "I think not, gentlemen. I fact, I am quite certain that these sharp and deep cuts were made by an ax, a very sharp ax, and they were made by someone very strong, quite powerful, who could wield an ax most effectively. A Woodman of some kind."

"A Woodman?" I asked in surprise.

"Yes, Watson, it appears that Dorothy has a companion and they have traveled down this very road but days ago. They came to this spot and the Woodman, cut these tree limbs and branches for some reason."

"What reason?" I asked.

"For fire wood," the Professor answered casually.

"Possibly," Holmes reluctantly admitted, then shook his head negatively, "No, not quite, I believe there is something more to it than just that. If you are cutting wood for a fire, why leave these cut branches laying here unused?"

"Well, it seems obvious that your Woodman cut more wood than he needed for a fire." I stated, not really paying all that much attention to this problem. This all seemed rather inconsequential to me—at the time.

"Perhaps," Holmes said thoughtfully shaking his head. "There is something more to this than what we are seeing here. I advise that as we walk through this part of the road, we should be alert for any trap or ambush."

I nodded, my hand already upon my revolver.

Professor Wonder just nodded agreement, his sharp eyes ever alert.

"Good, then let us continue walking," Holmes told us.

I took the lead and suddenly yelled out, "Oh! Whoa! What now!"

Then I quickly fell to the roadway as if tripped, or pulled down.

Holmes and the Professor rushed over to me.

"Watson!" Holmes shouted. "What was it?"

"I do not know. I was tripped by a branch of that tree—but where is the branch now!" I proclaimed in sudden shock and surprise.

It was then that they were upon us!

It was the most amazing thing I had ever been involved in. All the trees along both sides of the road suddenly flung their branches and limbs at us in an effort to stop our progress forward and to block our passage down the road.

"What is this?" I declared in anger, and then fear, for the trees were actually fighting us, using their limbs and branches to knock us aside, to push us back from the road, and to block our advance. It was most strange and also a bit terrifying.

"Most belligerent! Most Aggressive behavior!" the Professor stated in anger. "They are actually fighting with us!"

"Yes, some type of fighting tree, no doubt under the magic of the Witch," Holmes told us as he helped me up, and with the Professor, the three of us began to battle our way forward, down the yellow road, through the wild swaying limbs and branches of these strange leafy fighting trees.

We deftly fought off the long thick limbs and branches that tried to obstruct our path down the road. We knocked aside each impediment the trees put against us, then ran on moving further down the road. I wished we had that Woodman and his ax with us to cut down the parts of the trees that were fighting against us. This was becoming dangerous, perhaps even deadly, for the trees tried to hit us and knock us down, then sought to pummel us with their swaying branches and limbs. Some of these limbs were quite stout and thick. When they struck us, it was hard, and painful, and we were lucky that none of our trio had been seriously injured as yet. It was becoming most dangerous and I knew that our very lives were at stake. Now I knew how Dorothy and her companion had made their way safely through these trees—with the Woodman and his ax—but we had no powerful Woodman with a sharp ax with us.

However, we did have Sherlock Holmes!

"Follow me, gentlemen!" Holmes ordered us in a rapid tone of voice. "Walk quickly now, in single file behind me, down the center of the road here. That will diminish the reach of the tree limbs and branches to make contact with us."

We did as Holmes told us and it did in fact diminish the belligerent effect of these mysterious fighting trees. Most of the trees could not reach us with their limbs and branches. Those parts of the trees that were able to reach us, we quickly and expertly knocked aside and out of the way as we quickly passed them.

In an hour of furious battle we were beyond that particular grove of fighting trees and were once again walking down the road of yellow bricks.

"Yes, the land of Oz is certainly most magical and strange," Professor Wonder noted with a nervous smile that included a winning twitch of his bushy brown mustache.

"I wonder what else we shall find here," I mused in a thoughtful tone. "That was a most dangerous conflict I should not want to go through again."

"Indeed, Watson," Holmes stated simply as we continued to walk onwards.

I could see that my detective friend was very much concerned by the behavior of these belligerent trees, which was most unusual and did not fit in with his view of reality at all. Nor my own, to tell you the truth. It was all most perplexing.

"Are you all right, Holmes?" I asked my friend.

He had suddenly become quiet, thoughtful. I wondered what was on his mind now.

He told me, "Never better, Watson, but I must admit the behavior of the fighting trees in that forest is certainly uncanny. We must realize that some of the normal rules of reality and behavior that we are familiar with from our own world, may not necessarily play well here at all."

"Yes, Oz is a most magical place," the Professor reminded us.

"Yes, magic perhaps, but to me it seems just a lot of mumbo-jumbo, or it is all just a big humbug, or so I have thought all along," I replied carefully, adding softly, "at least until now."

"Yes, here in Oz, Watson, magic apparently does work," Holmes warned, and I could see the truth of that troubled him and upset his very logical mind. It was a difficult thing for him to accept, but accept it he did. For facts were always the forte of Holmes. Then he nodded and said, "Come along now, we have more of our journey to complete before we reach this City of Emeralds."

"Follow the road of yellow bricks!" I intoned caustically, recalling the Munchkin's advice to us, then I shrugged, and the three of us continued on our travels.

* * * *

It began to get dark as night was fast approaching and now we found ourselves moving along a thin and worn part of the yellow road that ran through a dark and gloomy woods, with withered black trees whose limbs clawed towards the sky, and a multitude of strange animal barks and growls coming at us from the darkness we passed all around us. Here, the gloomy trees had lost their colorful leaves and instead clawing branches rose up and above to form a thatch-like covering over the yellow road, so that the darkness was almost absolute as we passed down the roadway. It was spooky. I noted with care that this part of our travels could be dangerous.

"Stay alert, Watson," Holmes warned me as his eyes scanned the area around us with a deep intensity. "You might want to have your revolver handy."

"Of course," I replied and withdrew my gun and held it tightly and carefully in my hand as I noted many mysterious bright red and yellow eyes masking who knew what wild creatures that now stared at us lurking in the utter darkness just off the road.

"So long as we stay on the yellow road we should be safe," Professor Wonder informed us, "but do not stray from the road for any reason, gentlemen."

I nodded. I certainly had no intention of anything of the kind. I recalled one of Holmes' cases. Never had I felt such fear as when we walked upon the lonely moor at midnight in that dastardly case I would some day chronicle as *The Hound of The Baskervilles*—but this came close. It was that bleak and grim here. Much like the Great Grimpin Mire. Holmes spoke not a word, but he looked wary, much concerned.

"Have a care, gentlemen, we are being watched," Holmes informed us in a whisper. "This is a perfect place for an ambush."

"I see something lurking in the woods and the thick brush at the very edge of the road," I spoke up in a grim *sotto voce* to my companions. We all watched around us intently, looking into the gloom that surrounded us, but we could make out nothing.

"They are there certainly, all around us, Watson," Holmes told me and the Professor in a low thoughtful voice.

"Do you see them?" I asked in a nervous whisper.

"Not yet," Holmes replied softly, "but I can hear them. They are there, lurking in the darkness, hiding in the shadows for now."

"What are they?" I asked curiously.

Holmes did not reply, and we just kept walking forwards. Ever watchful. We quickened our pace considerably.

"What are they?" I asked again.

"I am afraid that we may soon find that out, Doctor," Professor Wonder replied in a grim whisper.

I nodded, held my revolver ready as my eyes strained to see into the utter blackness that surrounded us. I could make out nothing.

"Stay upon the road, gentlemen. Do not leave the road for any reason," the Professor warned us once again.

Then I saw them! They were looking at us most carefully. Intently.

"Sunflowers!" I stammered in incredible surprise. "Gigantic sunflowers!"

They were indeed very tall sunflowers, ten to twenty feet in height, and we could now see them more plainly since we had moved closer down the road and the moon light shone upon them. They were bunched up at the edge of the road on both sides. I felt that they could be dangerous. They appeared most intimidating and it may seem surprising that I was intimidated by a forest of giant sunflowers, however just coming through the fighting trees, it was most understandable.

"Holmes?" I whispered nervously.

"I feel it too, Watson. There is something most strange about these tall plants," he told us in warning. "This is most unusual. All of the giant flowery heads of these enormous plants are looking directly at us."

"What does it mean?" I asked, feeling a growing nervousness at the intense attention of these enormous plants. Were we in danger from them?

"Watson, Professor, have a care now. Move on briskly. Sunflowers always face East in the morning and always West in the evenings, but though this is evening, these plants are all facing us, no matter what direction they are located. See, they grow on both sides of the road, but all of them are facing directly upon us!" Holmes stated carefully, looking over the enormous plants most thoughtfully. "That is not possible."

"In Oz it may well be possible," the Professor stated ominously.

I could not figure it, but it seemed to me that the 'face' or 'heads' of the tall plants did seem to be following us, looking at us, maybe even listening to our words. It was very nerve-wracking. I told my feelings to Holmes. "Good observation, Watson, I believe you may be correct."

Suddenly we heard a deep sonorous voice call out to us.

"Are you minions of the wicked Witch?"

I looked aghast at Holmes and then the Professor, and they shot a look at the closest sunflower, a veritable giant, that seemed to have a face that had now formed in the dark center of the head surrounded by so many large yellow petals.

"What is that!" I asked in surprise.

"It just spoke!" the Professor added in shock, pointing at one of the plants. "That sunflower just spoke!"

"Impossible!" I stammered showing my confusion.

"Indeed, it did speak, gentlemen," Holmes informed us. Then he looked at the giant sunflower and replied in a calm firm voice, "My name is Sherlock Holmes and these are my companions Doctor Watson and Professor Wonder. We are traveling to the City of Emeralds to see the Wizard."

The giant sunflower bowed down it's massive head to get a better view of Holmes. It was a most amazing confrontation, to see Sherlock Holmes in conversation with an enormous sunflower. The other sunflowers all were turned in our direction and looking on most interestedly. I could hardly believe what I was seeing.

"Then you are not minions of the evil Witch?" the giant sunflower—who appeared to be their leader or spokesman—asked my companion.

"No, we are here to rescue the Doctor's niece, Dorothy. We are not under the command of the Witch, quite the opposite. We are her enemies," Holmes told the huge sunflower calmly. Then he added, "You and your fellow plants appear to be in some distress. Why is that?"

"Why?" the giant plant replied in a deep sigh, it's large yellow leaves drooping sadly. *"We see what the Witch's minions are doing to the red poppies, down in the valley, terrible, terrible! We are most fearful that they will seek us out next for the same treatment."*

Holmes nodded, "I see. Well, we are enemies of the Witch and you have nothing to fear from us."

There was a long silence, as if the plants were communing with each other. Then their leader spoke up more softly.

"Then you may pass down the road. We will not impede you."

"I thank you," Holmes told the giant sunflower, and the huge plant bowed most gracefully. Then all the other sunflowers gave Holmes the same respectful bow. It was quite amazing to see.

"Come now, gentlemen, let us continue our mission," Holmes told us, and the Professor and I quickly followed him down the yellow road. On the way, I took one last look back at the giant sunflowers and they did not seem so intimidating to me any more. They looked somewhat sad and even fearful. I felt sorry for their plight.

"I think that evil Witch has put them in some peril, Holmes," I told my companion.

"Yes, one more item in the ledger against her, Watson. Now, come along, let us move on quickly, we are nearing the city."

CHAPTER 11: THE JOURNEY CONTINUES

"I suggest we continue our journey away from this place immediately," Holmes ordered in a firm tone. He gave me a grim smile, "Come now, let us move briskly down the road and take ourselves away from here."

"Mr. Holmes is correct," Professor Wonder replied with a sage nod of his head, "Keep moving down the road. Do not stop on any account."

We heeded the Professor's wise words and did a rapid jog though the darkness down the road the remainder of that dark dreary night. It was a long hard night but we never looked back.

A few hours later the sun was just moving up into the brightly colorful Oz sky. We were tired from lack of sleep, but the fear we had felt the night before was still within us and kept us moving. We had now come to a hilly land in which the yellow road wound through like a large coiling snake.

When we reached the top of one of the taller hills I looked down into a bright red valley and then saw, far off in the distance, an incredible city—a gleaming bright sparkling white city of tall majestic buildings.

"The City of Emeralds," the Professor told me in a voice that was full of awe and wonderment, a feeling that I also felt viewing the distant city.

I looked at him curiously, then I asked, "But I thought the city was emerald green? Perhaps built of green marble or green stone?"

"Yes, that is the rumor, but not quite, Doctor," Professor Wonder explained with a sly grin. "We shall find out the truth about all that soon enough."

I nodded, letting that pass for the moment, adding in evident relief, "Then we have reached our destination?"

"Well, yes and no, Doctor," Wonder warned with a grim look to his face. "We still must get to the city. That could prove most dangerous."

"The Witch?" I asked him, but he did not reply right away. It had me wondering just what was in store for us now.

"Professor Wonder?" I inquired softly. I had the feeling that the Professor knew more about Oz than he was saying and I could tell from the look on Holmes' face that he thought so as well. Holmes was already looking intently at the valley below us. He seemed to find it quite fascinating.

The Professor then added, "You see that red valley below us?"

I did. It was bright red. It looked rather pretty.

Holmes was looking at it most intently too now, and nodded thoughtfully.

I said, "Yes, I see it, quiet a lovely valley full of little bright red flowers. The flowers appear as bright as newly spilt blood, almost like a red carpet set out to greet us."

"Not quite a greeting, Watson," Holmes said in a cold whisper.

I looked at him with some concern then, for I had learned well that things in this most magical of lands could be most dangerous and not at all what they seemed.

I asked, my companion, "I believe our path to the city runs right through that valley?"

"Yes, I believe it does," was Holmes' only reply.

The Professor explained, "Indeed it does, gentlemen, but that blood red valley is most dangerous. We must traverse that field of lovely deadly blooms before we can ever reach the City."

Sherlock Holmes nodded, "A poppy field. It is the red poppy I seek."

"Yes, and it can be deadly, Mr. Holmes," the Professor informed us.

Holmes noticed something in the Professor's manner, "You look perplexed?"

The Professor showed a bit of confusion upon his face and then replied, "The poppy field looks disturbed and it seems smaller than what Miranda showed me only weeks ago. It is most strange."

"Perhaps it was the weather?" Watson interjected, "It could result in a small crop now?"

The Professor shook his head, "Ironically, even as we have all come to Oz through the device of a cyclone, yet I have never seen any climate change in Oz. Not even rain."

"No rain?" Holmes asked thoughtfully. "None at all?"

"Never,' the Professor replied categorically. Then he looked at Holmes and said, "That field has been cultivated, for certain!"

Sherlock Holmes just nodded at that bit of information. "The Sunflowers were right. They were correct to be in distress, for they have seen the harvesting of the red poppies, and fear they are to be next."

"Your red poppy, Holmes?" I asked my companion, quite incredulous. "All the way from Oz?"

"Apparently, the very same, Watson. It appears we have found the source of the Red Poppy Menace presently plaguing London," Holmes informed me grimly.

"Can it be, truly? Here in... all the way from Oz?" I asked astounded.

"Indeed, Watson, we have found the source of the red poppy powder that has of late become such a scourge of the drug addicted in Greater London," Holmes repeated thoughtfully, and I wondered what he was thinking and so I asked him.

"You actually believe that this field of flowers is the source of the red poppy powder, Holmes?" I asked him surprised and confused how such a thing could be possible. I could not see how the powder from here, could be transported from this world, to our own. It seemed incredible, even impossible, but one thing I had learned in my time here in Oz, is that the incredible and the impossible often do not apply. Magic seemed to rule here with a steady hand and worked under it's own inexplicable rules.

"Yes, Watson, I am quite sure of it. The dread red poppy is a flower that makes a powder that I am sure is identical to that found in our world—but seeing it here in Oz—that is most strange. Certainly confirmation of communication between our worlds—"

"There are many strange things here in Oz, Mr. Holmes," the Professor stated simply.

"That is certainly true," Holmes replied briskly, ready for action and to get moving. "Now let us immediately make our way around this poppy field so that we can reach the city. I have no wish to travel through it. I am sure it could be deadly. There must be some way for us to go around it."

"Hold off for a moment if you please, Mr. Holmes. You can not go around the poppy field for it will take us many days out of our way, it is wide and vast, so traversing through it is quicker. However, that may be easier said than done without proper protection," the Professor informed us, and I wondered what he meant. "You see, breathing the pollen of the red poppy can be deadly. It will certainly put us in a trance-like state, unless we wear the proper protection devices, that is."

"Then we are stymied?" I stated grimly, "for we have no such protection."

"You do not—but I do! Fear not, my friends, for I had the foresight to carry with me three of these small breathing filters I built just for this situation. If we wear them we should be able to traverse the poppy field without any ill effects." the Professor told us with pride in his voice at his most timely invention. He took the devices out of his travel bag and showed them to us. We looked them over with great interest. They were rather small carbon filtered face coverings. "They prove quite useful in brush fires back home. They should work well here."

I nodded at the Professor, surprised but delighted by his preparation. "How did you know to bring them?"

"Miranda, gentlemen, I saw it in her crystal, so I took the precaution of packing three of these small filters with my personal goods, just in case we should need them," Wonder stated with a sly smile. "They are very small and light to carry."

"Well, done, Professor Wonder!" Holmes praised the fellow grandly.

"Well, we will be safe enough wearing these," Wonder added, handing us each one of his small filter devices. It was a compact device that covered the nose and mouth, and contained a carbon filled pouch to breath through. It stopped the red poppy dust from entering the mouth and lungs when we breathed. And it protected the eyes as well.

"This is a most wondrous and effective device," Holmes stated intrigued by the Professor's respiratory filter. "You are a most ingenious inventor. Now let us be on our way."

Now properly attired in our protective breathing apparatus, we began our travel down from the hills and into the thickest patch of the dread red poppy field that sprawled out below us.

"It is a very wide field, but not excessively deep, only ten or so miles. We should reach the city in a few hours if we walk quickly," the Professor told us.

We walked quickly, with Holmes taking small specimens and samples, even as he made notes along the way. He would write down short scribbled words upon his pad, as he said things like, "Most interesting!" or, "Aha, this is the missing piece of the puzzle!"

Three hours later we were out of the red poppy field and safe from the effects of any of the dust. We had no ill effects because of the Professor's wonderful filter. We took off our protective devices, once again breathing the fresh clean air of Oz, and continued on our way upon the yellow road to the City of Emeralds.

The magnificent city was close now, the bright lovely tall buildings each gleaming with differing hues of shiny white, and off-white, colors, not at all green or emerald in coloring as I had been led to expect. Nevertheless, it was beautiful and even awe inspiring, though I was still perplexed. It was a truly magnificent city, but it was certainly not an emerald green-hued city!

"That city is the home of the Wizard of Oz," the Professor told us as he led us forward towards what I could not even guess what was to come.

"Indeed," Holmes replied and he gave the Professor a knowing look that had me wondering what else had passed between them. If there was some secret that he held, Holmes had not, as yet, related it to me.

In any matter, I was utterly transfixed by the vision of the lovely city we walked towards that shone upon us in the distance. I could not think of any place, even our own Buckingham Palace, being more majestic for the home of such a powerful personage. A queen, or a wizard, the Wizard of Oz himself! I fear that I was a bit over-awed.

Holmes was his usual stoic self, patient, waiting to see what the future would bring—but I knew he was anxious to find Dorothy and bring her back home safely.

The three of us continued our trek until we reached a tall wall of smooth rock surrounding the glorious great white stone city, and we came to a large protective gate. We approached the gate carefully, for all things in Oz were often mysterious and magical, so that nothing was what it at first seemed to be.

CHAPTER 12: THE CITY
OF EMERALDS

There was a door set in the large gateway that led into the magnificent city. It was closed and securely locked shut. I knocked upon the door in the gate, but there was no answer. Holmes gave me a go-ahead nod, and I knocked again, more loudly this time, and finally a well-dressed short man who wore all green clothing—he even had the most amazing green hair topped by a red cap—opened the small spy door and looked down upon me most annoyed.

I was obviously surprised that such an odd-looking fellow would be the keeper of the gate into this wonderful city, but this was just another aspect of Oz I knew I would have to get used to.

"Who are you? What do you want here in the great City of Emeralds?" the green man growled loudly and he seemed quite agitated by the appearance of myself and my two companions. I noticed that he wore rather strange thick glasses that had green lenses, that rested upon a prodigious nose, that had the most elaborate set of mustachios growing out from under it.

"We want to enter the city," I stated, telling the green man firmly, he seemed to be some kind of civil servant, a gatekeeper, no doubt. "We have business with the Wizard who we are told lives here. Let us into the city."

"Business? Business with the Great and Terrible Oz, you say?" he blurted out, looking us over most carefully, his eyebrows raised in evident surprise, and his long thick mustachios seemed to move and twirl with rapt agitation.

"Well?" I prompted, trying to hold down my impatience.

"My good fellow," Sherlock Holmes spoke up now looking directly into the eyes of the gatekeeper and speaking in a firm tone, "The Wizard will want to see us, and especially this man here, I can assure you. For we bring him news from his home country. Professor Wonder here, is the brother of your Wizard—do you not see the family resemblance?"

I looked askance at Holmes, trying to figure out just what his game was. Had he made up this ploy? Or was it actually the truth? He had never shared such information with me. Could it be true that somehow Professor

Wonder was the brother of this Wizard fellow? I was as surprised by this bit of news as was the gatekeeper.

Professor Wonder did not ruffle his demeanor at all, but stood by solid and nodded most judiciously at Holmes and myself. He then added to the gatekeeper and spoke up proudly, "Yes, it is true. What Mr. Holmes has told you is the truth, though how he has figured it out, I do not know. Your Wizard, is my brother. With that in mind, I am sure my brother, your Wizard, The Great and Terrible Oz himself, will want to see me immediately."

The gatekeeper nodded knowingly and suddenly changed his tune. "So you are the brother to Oz? Why did you not tell me this before! That is a different matter altogether. Quite different! Come on in sir, come right on in. Give me a moment and I will unlock the gate, and you and your companions are most welcome to enter the city. I shall escort you personally to the Wizard's Palace. But here, first you must wear these special glasses. Without these spectacles the brightness and glory of the City of Emeralds would surely blind you."

The man then handed us each a set of thin-rimmed eyeglasses with green-hued lenses, just like the ones he wore. It was most strange, but we put them on as he instructed, and immediately everything in the City of Emeralds was colored to a deep bright green or emerald hue. Now the city and everything in it, including it's people, became emerald-hued and every shade of scintillating green. The city was truly all emerald green now and even more amazingly beautiful.

"Most strange, and quite amazing," I stammered looking around me at the tall lovely buildings that now were every tint of the color green.

"Yes, quite interesting, but also quite meaningless," Holmes remarked as he looked around him at the buildings and the people as well. Then he took off his glasses, and instructed us to do so as well. "We will not need these."

"Quite right, Mr. Holmes, interesting or not, it is just another slick trick from my brother, who calls himself the Wizard," Professor Wonder spoke up as he looked around him through the green lenses, and then took them off and put them away. He smirked with a grimace, "City of Emeralds indeed!"

"Nevertheless it is quite a lovely city," I added, as the gatekeeper unlocked the gate and now with flourishes of his hands and arms, bade us a grand entrance.

The gatekeeper saw that we had taken off our spectacles, and was most upset, "You are all welcome, however, you must wear the green glasses. It is a rule handed down to us by the Wizard himself! You must wear them!"

"It is of little consequence. We shall wear them as you wish for the present, now lead us to the Wizard immediately," Holmes spoke forcefully to the little green fellow now. I could see that my companion had lost his patience with this nonsense, but when the little green man tried to lock the glasses onto Holmes head, he would not allow that at all. Nor would I or the Professor. So that while we might wear the green tinted glasses, they were not locked onto our heads—as we later learned they were locked upon all the inhabitants of the city. It was most odd and disconcerting.

"I have the only key," the green man informed us with a sly grin.

"Then I think it best you turn it over to me, immediately" Holmes insisted, and such was the will of his personality and charisma, that the green man handed over his key to Holmes right away.

"Good," Holmes replied, pocketing the key. "I shall make use of this later. For now, take us directly to the Wizard."

The green man shrugged, "As you will. I grant you entrance into the City of Emeralds, however I must warn you that the Wizard has not been seen in quite some time... "

"And why is that?" Holmes asked right off, though he did not seem much surprised by learning this knowledge.

The green man shrugged once more, and just shook his head.

"It is obvious this man does not know what has happened to your brother," Holmes whispered to Professor Wonder. "We shall see what develops once we are inside the Palace and can make proper inquiries. For now, let us wear the green glasses and see the city just as your brother and the inhabitants see it."

The Professor nodded his agreement and we each put our green-hued glasses back over our eyes, and then passed through the gate into a most wondrous city.

We were immediately taken aback as we walked into the glorious green-hued city, to view a veritable magnificent collection of lovely tall buildings inhabited by a most beautiful and inquisitive people, all of whom were very brightly and colorfully dressed in green-hued clothing. In fact, everything was green. The glasses made that so.

The green man escorted us through the green streets and to a large emerald-hued stone palace that glittered in the green sunlight. Guards in green uniforms saluted us as we approached. I was most impressed, Holmes just smiled indulgently. Only Professor Wonder seemed to be looking at everything around him in a most serious light. I wondered why.

"My brother's favorite color, gentlemen," the Professor explained to us, "has always been green. Green is also the most soothing of all the colors of the rainbow. It exudes peace and serenity. It is most wizardly."

"So that explains the use of the emerald green color here," Holmes spoke up with a wry grin. "I suspected as much. Let us continue onward."

As we were escorted through the city I asked Holmes how he knew about the Professor and his brother. It seemed most mysterious to me, and I was a bit taken aback that he had not informed me about this information until this very moment.

"Watson, you look, but you do not see. All the evidence was plainly visible days ago," Holmes told me with a sly grin as we walked through the marvelous emerald-hued city soon to wait before the entrance to the Wizard's stunning green-hued palace—which the glasses we wore showed us. "Do you remember when we were in the Professor's home back in Kansas?"

I looked closely at Holmes, "Yes, of course I do."

"Well, at the time I noticed some interesting items on display there," Holmes explained with a coy look. "I saw two wizard caps in his living quarters. They were small and old, as if belonging to two boys from many years ago. When they were children. Then to solidly cement that fact, I spied an old photo of two boys who looked very much alike dressed as magicians—or might it be—Wizards? I knew one was our Professor, but it was simple to deduce who the other boy might be. Certainly his twin brother. Then when the Professor said he knew of somebody disappearing in a cyclone—and of his interest in Oz and cyclones—I surmised that his brother is, in fact, the Wizard here in Oz. They are, in fact brothers, two young boys whose parents put them on the circus and carnival show circuit with an act playing young magicians."

"I never imagined such a thing, Holmes!" I stammered. "I am rather amazed."

"So was I at the time, Watson," Holmes admitted dryly. "I suppose I should tell you now that Professor Wonder, is not even our friend's true name. I have not told him what I know of him yet, but you might well ask what it is?"

"I might? I certainly will!" I stated firmly, looking closely at my friend. He enjoyed these moments when he was able to explain what he had learned in his cases. However, these rare moments of candor by him were only done in his own time, and at his own pace, for Holmes did not ever want to—let the cat out of the bag, so to speak—before it was the proper time.

However, it was the Professor himself, who explained to us his story.

"I am not one of the Marvelous Wonder Brothers, Doctor," the Professor said in all sincerity and candor. "I use Wonder as my stage name now, and a most excellent name it is. Actually, I am one of the Marvelous Baum Brothers, Master Magicians and hot air balloon enthusiasts. I am Lyman Frank Baum, and go by the name of L. Frank Baum, often simply called Frank. My twin brother is Oscar Zoroaster Baum. His full name being Oscar Zoraster Phadrig Isaac Norman Henkel Emmannuel Ambroise Diggs Baum better known as O.Z., hence Oz, and Oscar is the man who has lately become known as the Wizard of Oz."

Holmes allowed a nod of his head then said, "Just as the Professor remarked earlier, use of the green-hued spectacles was a trick used by his brother to further his wizardly credentials. Just any city would never do for his grand wizardry—only an emerald-hued gleaming city would prove just the thing to have the locals believe in his magical powers. As the Professor already told us, green was his brother Oscar's, favorite color. So that mystery is solved, at least."

"But only if the people wear the green-hued glasses," I said finding the one flaw in the Wizard's plan.

"Well done, Watson, but if I am not very much mistaken it is a rule or law here that everyone in the City of Emeralds must wear the green glasses all the time," Holmes explained further, "and furthermore, they are locked on, so that the people can not take them off."

"Yes, I see. That is terrible."

"Well, I shall take care of that soon enough. I now have the key and shall set them all free of these silly spectacles, but in the meantime we must see the Wizard," Holmes told me thoughtfully. "If he is here."

I nodded a bit upset now at the realization of all this information. "Then it is just as the Professor told us, I was correct in my suspicions from the very beginning, and this is all just one big humbug!"

Holmes shook his head negatively, "Not exactly, Watson, for there is real magic here in Oz. So do not be too quick to judge. I am sure we will find the truth of things here, as time goes on, and it shall all balance out."

We were quiet for a moment as the Professor gave us a knowing smile.

"Quite a palace my brother has built here," the Professor told us allowing a cynical grin. "Now you know the story of the Baum Brothers, and even the City of Emeralds. My brother, Oscar, is a bit of a charlatan, but he means well and is a good man. He is apparently a very good wizard. I hope I shall see him soon. I am sure he will help us, if he can do so."

Holmes nodded and looked to the Professor with a wry grin, "You have figured everything out?"

"Yes, I believe I have, Mr. Holmes. Much as you have figured out that Oscar and I are brothers." Wonder told us with a knowing smile—I still thought of him as Professor Wonder and not L. Frank Baum. "Oscar came here from Omaha in his own hot air balloon, and he went missing years ago in a cyclone from the Nebraska State Fair. I looked for him for years. Then through Miranda I found out about Oz and saw that he was here. I saw other things about Oz as well. How did you now I am his brother?"

"Elementary, my dear Professor. I noted certain items from your boyhood in your house back in Kansas," Holmes explained with a knowing look, "as well as your intense study of cyclones."

"Well, I wish someone would tell me what you have figured out," I demanded diligently. I knew the two men were talking around some other matter. I suspected it was about how the Professor's brother, Oscar, had come to Oz and apparently become the Wizard. Then Holmes told me all about it.

Holmes laughed lightly, "Good Watson, there is no Wizard, he never really existed. There may be some machine or device to make it appear that he exists in the palace audience chamber, but there was never any actual Wizard in Oz. Not until now," Holmes stated simply. "You see Oscar came here to Oz and became the Wizard, then he had the City of Emeralds built."

"So what do you think has happened to my brother?" the Professor asked showing his concern.

"That is a good question. The fact that he is not here to meet us—*you*—is significant. He would certainly be informed of your arrival. Hopefully, he is just now in hiding from the Witch," Holmes added with a slight nod of his head, "which is probably a good idea. Or perhaps he is being held captive by the Witch's minions. Once the Witch is defeated, I believe he will be set free and all will be made well again."

"And if the Witch is not defeated, Holmes?" I asked the fearful question most carefully that was in all our minds at that time.

"Why then, Watson, we have no need to worry about anything ever again," Holmes stated simply as a dark look clouded his face. I knew that he was worried about failure and realized just how concerned he was about the problem and he spoke with the Professor closely about it.

I was listening to his words rather shocked and amazed, but I simply nodded my head accepting all that I had just heard. Apparently Holmes and Wonder had organized and planned what they would do well beforehand. Without my input. I was a bit taken aback by being left out of the planning stage of our operation, but was resolute that I would do all I could to help them. After all, our quest was to rescue my great niece, Dorothy, and bring her back home safely. So I was in for a penny, in for a pound, as they say.

Our escort, the gatekeeper, took us further into the Palace of the Wizard where more of our questions were to be answered.

CHAPTER 13: THE ROAD
TO OBLIVION

Holmes and I, joined by Professor Wonder, entered the depths of the Wizard's Place and were escorted into the throne room by a magnificently uniformed major domo. He was an officious looking fellow, also fully dressed all in green. He also had green hair and a long green beard. He was very serious. The room was empty.

"Where is my brother? Where is the Wizard!" the Professor asked the major domo.

"He is not here, sir. Whether he has left the Palace, or has been taken captive by the evil Witch, we do not know for certain," the man replied calmly. "I am sorry that I cannot help you gentlemen."

"We are here to seek his help to rescue Dorothy, my niece," I told the green fellow. "Do you know where he might be found here in the city?"

"Dorothy? Oh, yes, Dorothy, the young lady, neither she nor the Wizard are to be found here at all."

"What?" I asked confused.

"Dorothy left days ago and she did so with three companions," the man replied with calm determination.

"Ah, yes, companions. Now it is all making sense," Holmes spoke sharply. "Recall what we saw in Miranda?"

"Whatever do you mean, Holmes?" I asked perplexed, he always seemed to be a step ahead, as was his usual mode of operation. You would think that I had become used to him by now, but I had not.

"Dorothy traveled with three companions. There is other evidence I have discovered that we must be alert to. The ax marks on the limbs of the fighting trees, Dorothy could not handle an ax, but a Woodman surely could. That is certainly one companion that Dorothy came this way with," Holmes stated, then added, "but all left together."

"However did you deduce that?" I asked in wonder.

Holmes only gave me one of his enigmatic smiles, then replied, "We know that Dorothy is held as a slave of the wicked Witch of the West and we have come to the City of Emeralds to get the Wizard's help to rescue Dorothy."

"Yes, of course," I replied.

"They all left the city," the major domo added most distinctly.

"But where did they go?" I asked the green man, then looked over at Holmes and Professor Wonder for some answer.

"Unless I miss my guess—*and I do not ever guess, Watson!*—Dorothy and her three companions took their leave of the city some days ago in search of the Witch," Holmes told me, then he looked at me closely, "she is now a captive of the Witch of the West, as Miranda showed us only days ago."

The Major domo nodded, "Yes, that is correct, they left days ago, just before the Wizard himself had gone missing."

"So it appears my brother's disappearance, is intertwined with the mission of Dorothy and her three companions to seek out the Witch, and possibly my brother."

"Yes, and no doubt to confront her," Holmes added carefully, then he spoke sharply, "Quick, now, we have little time left, for Dorothy and her companions are in great danger. I am afraid we are very much on our own now! We must leave the city immediately and find them—before the Witch goes through with her plans!"

"Bravo, Holmes! I am with you, then let us be off right away," I stated full of enthusiasm now that the prospect of action was in the offering.

"And I shall come with you to help any way I am able," Professor Wonder stated grandly. "I have a feeling that the best way to help my brother, is to help you two gentlemen find Dorothy, and then defeat this Witch."

* * * *

So the three of us set forth immediately upon the road to the castle of the wicked Witch of the West.

"How do we find the lair of this Witch?" I asked Professor Wonder, and I caught a sly look play upon Holmes' lips, presaging some unspoken knowledge.

"Fear not, Doctor," the Professor told me with a grim smile, "once the Witch discovers we are coming for her, she will surely find us."

And with that ominous warning, we began our long trek down the road away from the City of Emeralds—to we knew not what destination—with me having no idea what we would find when we got there.

We walked on for many more miles. It was an arduous trek down a brick road that was not at all as nice as the road made of yellow bricks which we had followed to come to the wonderful city. This road was dark and twisted, seeming to me as if it were the road to oblivion. I feared what we might find there, but I was all for pushing on for the sake of my niece.

"Come now, Watson, and you too, Professor," Holmes told us leading the way at a brisk pace. "We must make all haste to reach the Witch's castle to rescue Dorothy and her friends as soon as possible, for I fear they are in terrible danger."

We followed Sherlock Holmes hour after hour until we came to a spot in the road that seemed to become more hilly up ahead. It appeared there was something upon the road. It looked most suspicious. I wondered just what it could be.

"There is surely something there," Holmes told us carefully as he moved off away from us. "I shall scout on ahead, in case it is a trap, and see what lies there upon the road. Wait here, but be alert. Watson, a steady hand upon your revolver might be in order."

I nodded as I watched my companion carefully walk forward, down the long road, to the mass that seemed to be strewn upon the road far ahead of us. I could not make out what it might be, but I watched closely as Holmes approached the area, took some time examining it, and then came back to the Professor and I.

"Holmes? What is it?" I asked with concern and curiosity.

"Yes, Mr. Holmes, what have you discovered down the road?" the Professor added showing his concern.

"It is a murder scene," he said simply, but ominously.

"Murder?" I stammered.

"Yes, perhaps. Certainly attempted murder, days ago. A great battle was fought up ahead, but it appears that Dorothy and her companions were victorious for all their enemies lay dead, and I did not see any of their bodies. Come, let us advance down the road to investigate more closely, but be careful for any trap. Steel yourselves, gentlemen, for the scene is not pretty."

I nodded, holding tightly upon the handle of my revolver.

We walked down the road and soon discovered what awaited us there.

It was in fact carnage, certainly some kind of a murder scene, with a bloody mass of fur and blood and...

"Wolves! They are wolves! And all are dead!" I stated in awe at what could only be termed terrible carnage.

"Yes all are dead. There are precisely forty bodies," Holmes informed me.

"How do you know that, Holmes?" I asked, looking upon the corpses, each one of the wolves had had it's head cleanly chopped off.

"I counted them."

"Oh, yes, of course," I replied feeling rather silly. Then I added, "but why did they cut off the heads of these wolves?"

"I think I can take a stab at that, Doctor," the Professor added quickly.

"Go ahead, Professor," Holmes instructed anticipating his words.

"It was the work of a Woodman. He carries a large sharp ax, does he not?"

"You are correct," Holmes replied with a wry grin. "Watson, take a closer look at the Wolves' wounds."

I nodded, took up my companion's suggestion and moved closer to examine the wolves better. That their heads had been cleanly cut off was plain enough, but then I noticed the manner in which the cuts were made.

"What does your medical training tell you, Watson?" Holmes asked me.

"Yes, of course, each wolf head was decapitated by one mighty blow, cleanly cut from a very sharp weapon, probably an ax. It had to be a Woodman and his ax who did the work."

"Yes, and when Dorothy and her little group were attacked by the Wolves, the Woodman stood forth and boldly killed all of the wolves with his mighty ax."

"So thankfully this battle went well, Dorothy and her companions won out. I see none of their bodies around the area," I stated carefully.

"Yes, Watson, you are correct. Come now, let us not dilly-dally here any longer. We have learned all we can from this site, let us continue down the road and see what we can find further on," Holmes said briskly.

We followed Holmes for another hour or two down that dreary road until we came upon another interesting site. I was the first one to notice what we had come upon.

"Crows, Holmes, a veritable massacre of big black crows," I stated in awe, as we looked upon the scene of dozens of dead black birds. This time I took a closer look at the bodies and spoke up before Holmes could instruct me to do so. I could see he was patiently waiting for my report. I picked up and examined the dead bodies of some of the crows most carefully. Checking their wounds most closely.

"What have you determined, Doctor?" the Professor asked curious.

Holmes as yet had said nothing.

"These crows were all killed by having their necks broken, obviously by someone with very powerful hands. There are exactly forty of them."

"Yes, and they were killed by someone with a severe aversion to Crows," Holmes told me thoughtfully. "Look at the strands of hay and straw about. What does that tell you?"

"Some kind of fight had happened here."

"Of course, and what else?" Holmes prompted me.

I looked over at him and then nodded, "Of course, it had to be—it was a Scarecrow. Scarecrows and Crows are most bitter enemies. Remember, we did see a Scarecrow in Miranda."

"Bravo, Watson! The Crows were the second group of creatures sent by the Witch to attack Dorothy and her companions, after the Wolves, but thanks to a Scarecrow this time, her minions once again were defeated. Our valiant Scarecrow killed all the Crows, breaking their necks with his powerful hands. This Scarecrow is another one of Dorothy's companions. There were no casualties we have discovered among Dorothy or her party, so they were successful in this fight as well."

"It is amazing, Holmes!" the Professor said in evident shock. "The Witch must be desperate indeed to send such creatures against a young girl."

"Desperate, but deadly," Holmes assured us. "We know she has Dorothy held as a captive in her castle now, but we are not so sure what happened to her three companions yet. The danger is still great. Come now, let us be away from here."

We followed Sherlock Holmes further down the road and while the Professor and I almost missed it, my companion immediately discovered what was there.

"You see them! Dead Bees, Watson! Very many of them," Holmes told me in a sharp tone. "Yet a third attack upon Dorothy and her friends by a swarm of Bees sent by the Witch. See the tiny bodies strewn dead upon the side of the road where they made their attack. You know my knowledge of Bees, and my studies of the Queen—I have even written a trifling monograph upon them—but in this case I need not go too deeply into my studies to see just what happened here."

Holmes took out his magnifying glass and examined the bodies of the dead Bees most carefully. "Just as I thought!"

"What happened here, Holmes? I admit I totally missed seeing the tiny bodies of the Bees, had you not pointed them out to me."

"Myself as well," the Professor added.

"This was the Witch's doing, her third attack upon our friends. The Bees must have come upon the Woodman first, he must have been out in front leading the group, and they all swarmed around him in what should be a deadly attack. However, this Woodman must be made of some type of metal to withstand such an attack. Now let me see, iron would be far too heavy for such a being, perhaps tin is more likely? Yes, it is tin, so we have a Tin Woodman! In any case the Bee stingers could not pierce his hard metal body, so their stingers were destroyed as you can see here through my looking glass, hence the Bees died soon afterwards. For any Bee that looses it's stinger is doomed to soon die."

"Yes, I remember, we saw such metallic men in the city," I recalled our visions of the City of Emeralds.

"Precisely, Watson!"

"That is amazing, Holmes!" the Professor spoke up.

"Not amazing, merely elementary," Holmes replied with a rather sad look down at the mass of dead Bees. I knew Holmes had a special affection and interest in Bees.

"I am sorry about them, Holmes," I said in a low voice.

"The Bees were used for nefarious ends, more slaves of the Witch, as were the Wolves and the Crows," he told me in a low growl. Then he nodded, adding in a better tone, "Innocents turned evil by a force beyond their control. Much like the Opium Zombies at home, Watson. Hopefully, her powers will not have us turn on each other. But be mindful of that. A great force is controlling these beings, and it is evil. Well, it appears that our friends have defeated the Bees as well, since there are none of their bodies present. So it looks as though they have been victorious once again. And yet I wonder... "

"That is good news, is it not?" I asked in a voice showing higher spirits now.

Holmes simply nodded, "Yes, but I fear each defeat made the Witch more desperate to bring down Dorothy and her companions. She has Dorothy already as a captive, so we know she has been successful, but what happened to her three companions? Dorothy is a captive in the Witch's castle, Miranda showed us as much, but where are her three companions? Come now, gentlemen, we must quicken our pace, for our four noble friends are in serious danger."

We saw the sense of Holmes' words so the Professor and I quickened our pace as we trudged on down that bleak dreary road.

We walked for another hour when Holmes voice rang out with a loud, "Hello! What do we have here?"

We were immediately alert, and carefully walked further down the road, and approached an area where we saw a truly terrible visage. It looked like a murder scene, but no murder scene I had ever encountered before.

"By Jove, Holmes, you are correct again! A Scarecrow and a Tin Woodman!" I stammered in awe, and then felt great sadness at what we had found.

We recognized what we had found as being two of Dorothy's boon companions, the Scarecrow and the Tin Woodman—or what was left of them! It was a terrible thing to see. They had been broken apart into many pieces and were apparently dead.

The Scarecrow had his arms and legs broken off and they were strewn all over the area, his straw and filling also strewn about so that his clothing was empty and lay limp on the ground. Just empty rags. I did not see his head anywhere. It was most odd.

Meanwhile, the poor Tin Woodman had his metal head, arms and legs all separated and detached from the main trunk of his body. He was totally dismembered and the parts of him were thrown around the grounds willy-nilly.

"Oh my! This is simply terrible!" I cried out in anger. "What has happened here!"

"Well, what has happened here, is that we were set upon by the dread winged monkeys!" A voice suddenly called out from behind the bushes. "Now, who are you, and can you help us?"

I looked around stunned by the strange disembodied voice, as if spoken by a ghost. I spoke up firmly, "I am Doctor Watson, and this is Sherlock Holmes, the famed detective from London, and that is Professor Wonder. And who might you be, just some ghost with a disembodied voice?"

"No ghost. I am the voice of the Scarecrow speaking from his head," the voice told us quite simply, and then I saw Holmes bring forth the head of the straw man out from where it had been thrown into the bushes off the road.

"Thank you," the Scarecrow spoke up to my companion.

"Think nothing of it." Holmes told the Scarecrow's head, looking into his eyes, then he turned to me he said, "Well, here he is, Watson, still able to speak, but he has no body left to go along with his head I am afraid."

"That is most distressing!" the Scarecrow's head told us.

This was utterly incredible and I blurted out, "What can we do about this, Holmes?"

"I must admit I am at a loss to say, you being a doctor and all, Watson, but were this happening back in London—and not here in Oz, there might be some way to remedy the situation."

The Scarecrow then answered in a wry tone, "That is correct. I believe that if you collect all my straw, and carefully stuff it back into my clothing, then you will be able to attach my arms and legs and head to my body, then I should be able to be put back together again."

Holmes looked at me quizzically, "Well, Doctor, you are the medical man, are you up to it?"

"Of course, Holmes, if it can be done I will be the one to put him back together again!"

"I will help him," the Professor added enthusiastically.

"Excellent, and I shall collect the parts of the Tin Woodman and see if I can put him back together again. I have some knowledge of mechanical devices and metallurgy so this should prove most interesting."

The three of us worked diligently upon the two poor creatures. It was not long before we had all the separate parts collected and the Scarecrow and Tin Woodman put back together again. They were sore and took some time getting accustomed to being back in one piece, but soon they were as good as new. Holmes found an oil can and oiled the joints of the Tin Woodman and this made him feel much improved. I looked at all this and just nodded, not being human, it seemed that the rules for such creatures were quite different here in Oz.

"Now, tell us, what happened here?" Holmes asked the two beings from Oz.

"It was terrible," the Scarecrow spoke up, and the Tin Woodman nodded his head knowingly. "The Witch sent Wolves, Crows and Bees against us."

"Yes, I know about them, we discovered their dead bodies on the way here. You did well in defending yourselves," Holmes stated with a look of admiration. "What happened after?"

The Scarecrow nodded, "After? Then the Witch sent her winged monkeys against us! They swooped down upon us from the sky and took us unawares. They quickly dismembered myself and the poor Tin Woodman. I saw them capture Dorothy and the Lion, and then fly away into the sky. Soon they were far away and gone. I assume they took Dorothy and the Lion to the Witch's castle."

"And little Toto, Dorothy's dog," the Woodman added.

"Yes, and that is the story of our defeat," the Scarecrow said sadly, trying to hold back tears for it was obvious he was worried about his friends. "Now we will never be able to save Dorothy, or that poor cowardly Lion."

"Lion? Ah, yes, the third companion," Holmes said, "now a slave of the Witch, taken away by the winged monkeys we saw in Miranda."

"Well, they shall never be saved now!" the Scarecrow said in grief, and if a scarecrow could in fact cry, then I was sure that what I was seeing streaming down his face were a river of tears.

"Never say never, Scarecrow!" I told him boldly, for my blood was up at seeing the evil the Witch had done to these three companions, and that she now had my helpless niece securely held prisoner in her clutches. "You and the Tin Woodman join us, and we will travel to this Witch's castle and rescue Dorothy!"

The Scarecrow and Tin Woodman happily agreed to my proposal.

Then I looked carefully at my detective friend, "Is that not correct, Holmes?"

"You said it perfectly, Watson. Come now, gentlemen, let us be off, to find this evil Witch and bring her the comeuppance she so earnestly deserves!"

CHAPTER 14: AMBUSH!

The five of us now walked on the dark winding road for many more hours through one of the bleakest lands of Oz. We were on high alert and walking close together for defense, should any enemies attack us. As we walked, the Scarecrow and Tin Woodman told us all about their previous adventures. How they had come to meet Dorothy, the Wizard, the Witch, the Queen of the Field Mice, and all the various friends and foes in this magical land. It was an amazing story, worthy of a book all on it's own.

We traveled onwards. I was ever wary of a trap or ambush, as Holmes had put me onto the alert for just such an eventuality. So with that in mind, I kept my hand upon the butt of my revolver ready for any contingency that the wicked Witch might thrust upon us. However, I saw absolutely no indication of what was to come, nor the shape and manner of the attack, nor how we would face it. Oz still held many surprises for me.

So we continued to walk onward towards the Witch's castle. Holmes and I busy in conversation with the Scarecrow, all ever vigilant, while the Tin Woodman held up the rear holding his large ax menacingly and ever ready. The Professor walked at his side.

Suddenly I heard loud terrifying sounds from behind me. Holmes and I jutted sharply around to see an incredible sight. The very ground seemed to be shifting and moving upwards, opening up in vast crevices. Everywhere the ground was in turmoil, lifting and roiling sharply upwards.

"What is this!" I cried out admittedly terrified. "Is it some kind of earthquake?"

"No, Doctor, but it is certainly the work of the Witch!" the Scarecrow warned us sharply, and I did not doubt it.

"Quickly," Holmes ordered, "form a defensive circle, we are under attack! Watson, be ready with your revolver!"

"What is it?" I asked holding down my fear now.

"I do not know yet," Holmes told me, which made my concern grow, for if he did not know what was happening here—but we did not have long to wait to find out.

I did not have to be told we were under some form of attack, but as I watched what was transpiring before my eyes, I realized that nothing was at all what it seemed to be. That we were under attack, was a foregone conclusion, but the shape and manner of that attack was what was so incredible to me that I did not see how we could put up any defense against it. Something was making it's way out of the ground to come up at us!

Finally we saw what it was, the face of our new enemy.

"Ants!" I shouted in fear. "They are ants!"

"Yes, but there are very many of them!" the Professor stated nervously.

"There must be millions of them!" the Tin Woodman spoke up, and it turned out he was correct.

"Ants, and they are everywhere!" the straw man shouted out in terror and warning. And he was correct as well, the ants were pouring out of the ground in massive swarms. They shook the very ground under our feet. They were small in size, but there must have been many millions of them— so they were very powerful and they came at us rapidly. I knew they would be thrust upon us very soon. We were already being bitten on our feet by the sharp pincers of what must have been advance scouts of the swarm.

"Run! Now!" Holmes ordered in a loud command, and all of us sped down the road doing our best to get away from that horrible ravenous horde. Then Holmes ordered, "Quickly, we must find a place to hold these creatures at bay!"

I knew that my revolver was useless against so tiny an enemy—and so large a number of attackers. Each of the ants was the length of my finger-nail, small in size, some type of fire ant, I assume, but each had large sharp pinchers. I knew they were seeking to swarm over us by the thousands, and that if they were able to accomplish that feat, they could devour us in minutes. It appeared we had no defense against them.

"We are doomed!" I shouted terrified by the tiny creatures as they came ever onwards at us. I saw no way out of this situation and looked over at Holmes, whose face was cold and stern.

"Hold fast, be patient, Watson!" Holmes told me, and his words did much to bolster my shaky manner. He now led us away from the swarm, apparently trying to find a good place where we could hold up safely. If such a place existed.

Nevertheless, I used my revolver and got off few quick shots into the attacking horde, but without any effect. The ants did not react to my weapon at all. I was most distressed to discover this, but not surprised. We followed Holmes down the road and he had us form up in a small defile that seemed to offer some defensive possibilities.

"Watson, my friends," Holmes told us quickly, "I am afraid that we shall be overrun soon, but we can make our last stand here, and bravely fight them off as long as we are able. Quickly gather up all the dry brush and branches that you can find and bring it here right away."

"What are you up to, Holmes?"

"I think I know. You know I am afraid of fire, but I am with you in this, Mr. Holmes," the Scarecrow shouted firmly and quickly got to work. I was surprised that he had guessed at what my detective friend had in mind. He was a rather sharp minded individual after all, although I do not believe he knew it.

"Yes, we shall fight them off as long as we can," the Tin Woodman added, swinging his ax with menacing wrath at the oncoming horde of ants. He then used his ax to chop large branches into smaller ones, making more manageable pieces of wood that we all gathered together.

I worked furiously to help make a barrier of sticks and dry leaves, "I am with you, Holmes…until the end!"

"I as well!" the Professor added, bringing over a pile of wooden branches.

"Bravo! No one could ask for more loyal or brave companions than you four, but we are not ended yet," Holmes told us with a bold confidence that I did not feel.

Then after ordering us to gather up all the brush and twigs that surrounded our area before the ants overran us, Holmes had us set them upon the ground around us in a wide ring. Then he set them ablaze. The fire burned brightly. The dry twigs, branches and small logs burned most easily and the ring of fire worked itself bright and hot to keep the ants at bay. It was almost magical.

"You saved us, Holmes!" I shouted with evident relief.

"Not precisely, good Watson," he told me in a stern tone, looking at me and our companions a bit too seriously. "The fire will cause the ants to keep back for some period of time, or until it burns itself out. What I have done is buy us some time, that is all. When the fire burns itself out, I am afraid that we will be at the mercy of the ants. I am sorry, Watson, I am sorry, my friends, but this is the best that can be done at the moment."

I nodded, realizing the deep predicament we were in and that there seemed no way out of it for us now. Dorothy's two friends nodded grimly, knowing that our quest would soon be at an end and the Witch would be victorious. Professor Wonder just put a hand reassuringly upon my shoulder and gave me a grim smile.

"Good show, Watson, Good show, Holmes," the Professor told us with a sad grin.

The ants continued to come on in a massive horde, a gigantic swarm of millions upon millions of the tiny red fiends in great piles that surrounded us, and surrounded the ring of fire we kept stoking to keep it as hot and raging as possible, waiting. They did not have long to wait.

"Holmes... ?"

"I know, Watson, the fire is slowly diminishing, soon it will burn itself out."

"Soon?" I asked softly.

"Yes, far too soon, I am afraid," Holmes replied with a grim look.

I nodded, looked over at the Scarecrow and the Tin Woodman, both were calm and patient, awaiting the inevitable. Professor Wonder was stoic, as was Holmes.

"Well, it rankles me no end that the wicked Witch will win! I can not accept this!" I stated in loud blistering words of bold defiance. "It is not right, and it should never be thus! There must a some way for us to escape this trap?"

"Ever the optimist, eh, Watson?" Holmes told me with a grim, but knowing smile. That smile told me he had not yet given up. It seemed he knew something, but was loath to say it as yet.

"What is it, Holmes?" I asked my friend impatiently, for I knew him and his many moods, and felt that something was indeed in the offering.

He looked at me then with a sly grin, "Perhaps we are not as lost as we may think? Perhaps someone has seen our fire and may come to aid us?"

I looked askance at Holmes, and he called *me* an optimist? I told him bluntly, "I appreciate your good words of optimism, but this is Oz, we are in the middle of nowhere, and there is no one here who can help us."

"We shall see, Watson," Holmes told me mysteriously.

I could not accept his words. I was defeated and deflated at the realization of our grim situation. A situation growing worse by the minute. I looked at Holmes for some hopeful words or action, but he was silent and I shook my head in despair.

The fire was burning ever lower now. It would not be long before the flames would be out. Then the ants would come and overwhelm us. It would be a quick but very painful death. I could see considerable agitation among the swarm of ants surrounding us. There appeared to be some commotion coming from the back of the ant swarm, which I assumed was the pressing hunger of the ravenous creatures in the back, pushing towards those in front of them, anticipating the coming feast. They seemed to be pushing the others forward. I felt like the blue-plate special at a four star Regent Street restaurant.

I sighed heavily and looked over at Holmes for some sign of hope. He and I, and the Professor would offer the ants a small enough meal, but at least the Scarecrow and the Tin Woodman would not become food for the swarm—and the Tin Woodman being made of metal might yet prove impervious to the ants. It did me some good to know that perhaps at least one of our little group might yet survive this horrendous attack and save Dorothy.

The fire was burning lower still. The ant swarm seemed to be just about ready to hurl itself upon us, the power of a great pushing and shoving by the swarm from behind was incredible. I wondered just what was going on back there. Then I saw it!

It was another swarm!

"More ants? What gives now!"

"Look closer, Watson!" Sherlock Holmes told me in a mysterious tone.

This time I saw it clearly! It was, of all things, mice! Many millions of small field mice had surrounded us—and the ants—and the mice were falling upon the ants and devouring them in huge gushing mouthfuls. I realized that this attack of the mice had been going on behind the ants for quite a while. Now the mice had worked their way through the massive ring of ants and were attacking the ants in front of the fire that surrounded us. The fire was getting lower and lower. I wondered if there would be enough time before the ants could come at us.

"Field mice, Watson!"

"Yes, but... ?" I was utterly astonished by the sight, but hopeful, seeing as it appeared the mice had come to our aid. Or had they?

The battle between the field mice and the fire ants went on for many minutes, the mice eating through the ants surrounding us so that they could not continue their attack upon us. The mice attacked with ravenous abandon. I had not thought such tiny creatures could be so aggressive.

It was not too long before the battle was over and the last of the ants had been eaten by the vast army of field mice. I looked at the results with amazement, our protecting ring of fire had finally gone out, and we now found ourselves surrounded by a massive army of field mice. They looked at us with tiny red eyes. There must have been a million of them. It was astonishing.

"Now what?" I asked Holmes, most curious and growing quite nervous that we had merely exchanged one enemy for another.

"We shall see soon enough, I am sure."

Holmes words proved to be true, for moments later the million field mice that surrounded us made a pathway. Then I saw a larger, older mouse regally walk through them. The Scarecrow and the Tin Woodman cheered in joy. I wondered what it was all about, then I remembered their story about how field mice had aided them in their first trek to the Witch's castle with Dorothy many days ago.

"We are saved!" the Scarecrow shouted in joy.

"The Field Mice have come to our aid once again!" the Tin Woodman stated victoriously.

Then the straw man stepped forward, and bowed deeply to the mice.

"May I present the Queen of the Field Mice," the Scarecrow explained in a voice that rang true with victory. "We welcome you, Your Majesty, and we thank you."

The Queen of the Field Mice bowed to the straw man, "I thank you, Sir Scarecrow, for I know that you and your companions are on a mission to rescue Dorothy, and I and my subjects are here to help you as we are able—in our own small way—to thwart the wicked magic of the Witch who has used so many poor creatures as ourselves for her own foul ends."

"Thank you for coming to our aid, Your Majesty," I told the small mouse queen, looking down at her where she stood upon the ground in front of me. I looked over at Holmes incredulous with surprise, "You knew?"

"I surmised, after recalling something the Scarecrow had told me of their earlier adventures here," Holmes told me with a nod of his head. "I was sure that the fire would get the attention of the Field Mice, and they would certainly investigate it, but I was not certain if they would get here in time. We are lucky that they did."

The Queen of the Field Mice came over to my companion then.

Holmes picked her up gently in his hand, and she allowed it.

"Sherlock Holmes, I presume?" the Queen said with a glowing smile.

"At your service, Your Majesty," Holmes told her with all sincerity and in a humble tone I had rarely seen him exhibit. He held the tiny mouse Queen delicately in his large palm up to his face, so that they could look at each other, eye to eye. "Thank you, and your subjects, for your assistance."

"You are most welcome. When Boq, a Munchkin child, told me a friend of Dorothy's was in distress, we came to help and saw the fire. Now fulfill your mission, Mr. Holmes. Rescue Dorothy, and that poor terrified Lion," the Queen told my companion in a lilting tone, adding, "and if you can do so, please kill the wicked Witch of the West. Her wickedness grows with every passing day. I see she is working with other forces to take over the entire land of Oz and make her foulness supreme here."

"What else do you know of this 'other force', Your Majesty?" Holmes asked the Field Mice queen most interested now by her response.

"The Witch has many minions, even some evil little Munchkins she has twisted to do her bidding. They control the Winkies who collect the red poppy flowers for some reason. We are scared of her, she has always been wicked but it seems she has some unknown motivation now to take over Oz and make it her own. We must not allow this. Perhaps she has some other ally? We do not know for certain, but I feel it, and she is more powerful than ever."

Wonder then said, "Perhaps the Queen is correct, Mr. Holmes, as I have seen an Englishman in Miranda, but until this moment I did not understand what she showed me or what it might mean."

"I thank you, Your Majesty. My companions and I shall do all we can to make that wish come true," Holmes told her offering a wry smile.

The Queen of the Field Mice nodded, then gave a queenly bow, and told us all, "Then by Our leave, be on your way, gentlemen. I am happy that I and my subjects could be of assistance once more in your noble quest."

"Thank you," I told her, adding with deep meaning, "You saved all our lives."

"And you came to our world to make it a better place, Doctor Watson," the Queen told me, "thereby I and my subjects commend you, and your companions as well."

We left the Queen of the Field Mice soon afterwards and our small group of five, lead by Sherlock Holmes, continued our journey along the road to the castle of the Witch of The West.

CHAPTER 15: THE WITCH'S CASTLE

The totality of what the Queen Mouse told us of the evil forces arrayed against us weighed heavily upon my companion's mind and I could see his concern as the five of us approached the castle of the wicked Witch of the West. We saw guards that patrolled outside the entrance to the castle and in front of a draw bridge, that was now down. We were informed by the Scarecrow that these were the Winkies, they had once been skillful tinsmiths and goldsmiths, but had been enslaved by the Witch. They were now the Witch's personal guards, and while they had once been normal decent beings, under the Witch's evil power they had become twisted in their obedience to her and her wicked aims, making them dangerous creatures. They came from a village called Tottenhots out in Winkie country.

"Do not let the name Winkie fool you," the Scarecrow told Holmes and myself. "They are the Witch's soldiers and they can be dangerous. They are skillful tinsmiths and they carry dangerous blades they use in their work, which are even more deadly than the ax carried by our tin friend here."

The Tin Woodman nodded in agreement.

"Yes, I see that," Holmes said softly looking at the Winkie guards and their weapons carefully, "and you are right, Scarecrow, those blades look quite sharp."

I nodded very concerned about this when I saw the guards. They certainly looked menacing and fearless, and probably deadly. They wore armor-like uniforms and helmets, and had yellow tinged skin that gave them a weird glow. They constantly patrolled their posts in front of the castle, almost as if they were automatons. Under orders, or the dark magic, of the Witch, no doubt.

"They do look quite formidable," Holmes stated watching the Winkies intently.

"Is there no way we can get beyond them?" I asked Holmes rather hopelessly as I noted their position blocking the gate. The guards seemed to be most effectively barring us from entering the castle. "I am afraid the Scarecrow's secret doorway is not attainable with all these guards here."

"We will find a way inside," Holmes spoke up softly as we watched the marching soldiers. The five of us were huddled unseen behind a large outcrop of rock watching the guards march below us, then we saw one group change position with another group. It was a changing of the guard most likely. We looked down upon them, watching them intently, looking for an opening or opportunity.

I saw Holmes nod with a wry smile as he watched their movements closely. I could tell he was planning something.

"This may just be our opening," Holmes stated carefully.

Holmes soon made a motion to get the attention of myself and the Scarecrow. "We can work our way down these cliffs over to those rocks over there. Then we might be able to dart towards the bridge, and under it, while the guard's backs are turned and they march on by. It might just work if we can do it quickly. See, they have their backs to us as they march to the gate, that is just the opening we need. If we are quick, we can get around them and under the bridge, and then access to the Scarecrow's secret doorway."

The Scarecrow liked the plan and said so. "Yes, Mr. Holmes, I believe that will work, but we must move quickly and time our movement so the Winkies do not see us coming up behind them. I am sure it will work."

I had my doubts, but there seemed nothing else to do about it.

Professor Wonder thought it was a grand idea. Of course, he would!

"I hope the wicked Witch is not looking for just such a plan of attack from us," the Tin Woodman added the statement with caution, and I agreed with that. "She has only one eye, but it is telescopic, so she can see far and wide and must know we are coming. She may even be watching us now."

Holmes nodded sagely, then said, "our Tin friend may be correct. The Witch can see us if she is looking for us, but she has not sent any attackers after us since the fire ants. I wonder why? Perhaps she is otherwise occupied? On the other hand, it may be that she has set a trap for us here, obviously an ambush, and she is waiting for us to approach, to come to her, so we must remain alert."

"The Scarecrow, the Professor and I, were eager, and the Tin Woodman nodded and hefted his ax ready. The four of us spoke up in a firm voice, "For Dorothy!"

"For Dorothy!" Holmes repeated softly with grim determination. "Now, I see the guards have just turned their backs to us, so we have bare moments, let us move quickly!"

Then Holmes and the Scarecrow led us down the sharp defile and quickly behind the unknowing Winkies. The five of us soon slipped unseen under the lowered bridge, and holding onto the bridge over our heads with our hands, we were able to move across the underside to the castle side of the moat. Here we landed upon a thin ledge and there before us was a small secluded doorway.

"It must be locked, surely," I stated cautiously. I tried the handle and the door was indeed locked. "Now how do we get inside?"

The Tin Woodman just smiled, hefted his ax and slammed it own upon the handle and the door flew open as if by magic.

"Good work, my Tin friend," the Scarecrow stated with a smile, then the five of us quickly entered the Witch's castle.

Soon we were well inside the Witch's hold. This was her most secure place, a place she never would believe anyone would willingly try to break *into*—only to escape *from*. It was a grim dark castle that oozed fear and dread menace. I could hear the other groups of guards nearby as we trudged away from them and carefully went further and further into the castle.

"Well, now that we are inside," Holmes asked quickly, "tell me now Scarecrow, where would the Witch keep Dorothy? There must be some prison or dungeon here, I presume?"

"Yes, Dorothy may be held captive there in a prison cell, but she also may be kept in the upper chambers where dwells the wicked Witch—her private rooms," the Scarecrow told us. "How are we to be sure where Dorothy will be found?"

"The dungeon, I think not," Holmes considered it for a moment, then rejected the idea, telling us confidently that he knew his criminals, and the wicked Witch was nothing if not a criminal; one who also had some powers of magic. "The Lion may be held in a cell in the dungeon, however, Dorothy will be in the Witch's private rooms. She will want to keep Dorothy and those silver shoes close by. We will seek these rooms first, then investigate the rest of the castle, and free the Lion later."

"Then follow me," the Scarecrow told us and our brave little group of five intrepid rescuers marched single file down narrow stone steps, through rough hewn corridors cut out of solid rock, to a place in the upper level of the castle where the Witch's private rooms were located. We reached a locked ante room below the Witch's rooms and heard a young girl crying. I knew at once it was Dorothy.

"Make haste," Holmes told us, for he knew we had little time left before the guards would be coming to take up their post. "Break down the door!"

"Dorothy? Dorothy?" the Scarecrow whispered frantically.

"Dorothy? Are you there?" I asked in a low tone.

"Scarecrow? Is that you?" the voice of a young woman came back franticly to us from within the room.

It was Dorothy!

The young girl cried out in sheer joy, "Yes! I am here!"

The Woodman quickly broke open the door with his most effective ax and we quickly ran into the room!. Dorothy was inside alone, and she seemed to be hale and hearty. I noticed that she still wore the silver shoes upon her feet. The Witch had not taken them from her yet.

"Oh, I am so glad to see you all! Scarecrow and Tin Woodman, but what of the Lion? So good to see you, but who are these three gentlemen?"

Dorothy asked rather confused but most happy now that help had arrived. She looked at us both most closely.

"I am Sherlock Holmes of London, and this is my friend and your uncle, Doctor John Watson, and I believe you know Professor Wonder. We are here to free you, but we must make haste and get out of this place immediately before the guards return or the Witch is alerted."

Dorothy looked at Holmes, then she looked over at me curiously and the Professor. "Great Uncle John, is that really you? Can it truly be you after so many years? All the way from London?"

"It is I, my girl, and we are all here to rescue you," I told her most joyously.

"And Professor Wonder? You are here too?"

"Hello, little lady," the Professor told her with a happy smile.

"You are free now, Dorothy!" the Scarecrow said in a joyful voice, that the Tin Woodman joined in on, he was showing some tears of joy.

Dorothy cried in relief as she walked out of the cold stark room. "But what of the Lion?"

"We believe he is in the dungeon below the castle. We shall free him soon.""Then come Toto, our friends are here to rescue us, and we must leave this place right away," Dorothy spoke up in joy, and her little dog, who I had not noticed until now, barked softly and then she picked him up as she quickly walked out of the room and down the hallway with us all.

"We can take you away from here to safety, Dorothy," the Scarecrow informed her.

Dorothy suddenly shook her head. "No! I must kill the Witch so the Wizard can grant our wishes. The Wizard said so."

"There is another way, Dorothy," Holmes told the young girl. "You do not have to kill the Witch to be free of her. However, the Witch is working with someone else, I am sure now."

"Someone else? You mean someone from Kansas?" I asked curiously.

"No, Watson, it is someone from London," Holmes told us and then I knew that could prove most disastrous. I looked at Holmes carefully curious.

"How can that be? How can anyone from our world... " I asked him, but he did not reply right away.

Sherlock Holmes just shook his head in quiet dismay, as if something that he had suspected for too long—but that had seemed impossible—might now prove to be true.

Holmes?" I insisted in a low tone.

"Very well, Watson," and Sherlock Holmes looked at me intently and uttered only one word that explained it all and made my nerves run cold with dread, "Moriarty."

"Are you certain?" I stammered in disbelief. "I thought he was dead?"

"Yes, well, apparently that is precisely what he wants us to believe. Somehow he has devised a way to contact the Witch here and the two have been working together on some scheme. I am sure now that it involves the red poppy. Moriarty may have a crystal ball, such as the one Professor Wonder had in his house. Remember poor Miranda? I assume the Witch has such a crystal globe here in her castle as well."

"She does, Mr. Holmes!" Dorothy spoke up quickly, "I saw it! Also some type of magical mirror. I saw them when she had me brought up there days ago, people come and go through it somehow."

Holmes nodded, "Then that is it! Our portal no doubt! We must find it and render it useless to her. Now that the Wizard, Professor Wonder's brother, Oscar, is missing, there is no one here in Oz to hold the Witch in check—and no one to stop Moriarty from oozing his snakelike coils of crime into this innocent world and poisoning it—as he has done in our own world. I fear greatly with him running amuck in London spreading this red poppy poison to the weak and ill there, and God alone knows what he might do if left to his own devices here in Oz!"

I shuddered at the very thought of that.

Holmes' words gave us all much food for thought. He continued in a firm voice, "Watson, you and I have important work to do here, as does Dorothy and her friends, so let us follow her to the upper floors of this castle, to the private apartments of the wicked Witch of the West, and to destroy her crystal ball—but protect that mirror at all costs! That should render her and her power impotent. Lead the way, Dorothy!"

"Come quickly, Mr. Holmes, Uncle John, and you Professor Wonder," Dorothy told us in a rushed voice, along with her two companions, who were now quickly following behind us. She added, "The Witch has her apartment on the top floor of the castle—she also has her crystal globe and magic mirror there. She tried to terrify me with her plans of revenge for killing her sister. But what she really wants is the silver shoes that I am wearing upon my feet now, the same shoes that came from the body of her dead sister. The Witch of the North told me to put them on the first day I came to Oz, and to keep them upon my feet—and never take them off—for they hold some magical charm. The wicked Witch tried to get the shoes from me, but she could not touch them, and she could not kill me to take them because the Witch of the North gave me a protective kiss upon my forehead. So the wicked Witch is stymied from harming me for now. She said she would do me deadly, but these things must be done with the utmost delicateness."

"The ways of magic," Holmes said completely understanding, as we all ran up steps to the top floor of the castle. "Continue, please."

Dorothy nodded, "Anyway, the Witch told me she would need to think upon her revenge upon me, for she wanted to make sure it was the most terrible revenge she could ever think of to perform upon anyone. She was just trying to scare me—and she did. I know now it is these silver shoes she really wants. And she has forestalled her revenge against me while she considers the best way to take the shoes from me—for she fears the reaction from the magic they possess should it work against her."

"Why has she not simply taken them off your feet?" I asked my niece.

Dorothy explained carefully, showing us the shoes more closely. They appeared to be rather standard woman's shoes with low heels and a bright silver coloring. "I believe she is trying to trick me into giving them to her. As I mentioned, I was given a protective kiss by the Witch of the North, so the wicked Witch is most wary of that."

Holmes spoke up then in a firm voice. "Whatever happens never remove those shoes from your feet."

"That is what the Good Witch told me, Mr. Holmes."

"Then heed her wise words," Holmes added sternly.

"I am so sorry you had to go through all this trouble, Dorothy," I told my young niece.

"Yes, my dear," Professor Wonder added offering her a sweet smile.

"It is all fine, Uncle John, Professor. Now follow me," Dorothy told us and we followed this brave young slip of a girl to our encounter with the dread wicked Witch of the West.

We moved quickly through the Witch's castle, up stairs and winding ramps, and soon reached the top floor level where the Witch's private apartment was located.

"That is it, her private chamber is through that heavy door at the end of this long hallway," Dorothy told us plainly. "See it there?"

I nodded, it seemed simple enough, but as I have learned, things are not often that simple here in Oz.

I saw her room was blocked by a huge sealed double-door, thick heavy oak-like timber held up with large iron hinges and thick metal bolts. It looked quite formidable. There were no guards, and that seemed most odd to me, for I had expected some kind of trap or ambush as Holmes had mentioned—then I heard the sound. It was guttural, animal, and it was most bestial, very dangerous and... it seemed to come from something that was invisible.

"It is The Hound!" Dorothy informed us, suddenly fearful now.

"What is 'The Hound?'" I asked, my curiosity quickly overtaken by an most sinister and ominous feeling of dire dread.

"It is a giant invisible hound that the Witch has placed there on guard outside her doorway," Dorothy warned us in a careful tone as she outstretched her arms to hold us all back from advancing any further. I looked ahead but could see nothing there, but something was certainly there. I could hear it breathing. Something very dangerous, and very big, I was certain.

What was it? What could it be?

Was it really a giant invisible hound? It seemed impossible. I looked again at the end of the corridor but could see nothing there.

"It is a giant hound, Holmes!" I spoke up to my friend nervously. "Only this one is apparently invisible."

"Yes, Watson, a most interesting challenge, but we have dealt with similar creatures before, have we not?"

I was instantly reminded of the hound of the Baskerville's problem, one of my friend's most trying cases, about a giant ravenous beast that was one of the most deadly creatures we had ever encountered. I felt a chill overcome me. Was this just one more indication of the connection between this world and my own?

I nodded, there seemed little to say upon the matter. I just wondered what Holmes had in mind to defeat this giant hound. While we had indeed dealt with creatures like this before—we had never dealt with anything quite like this.

"I am unable to see it," the Tin Woodman added waving his ax menacingly before him, as if to ward off any attack. An attack he could not see.

"It will be upon us in a moment, if we do not run," the Scarecrow stated, and the Woodman, though brave to the point of foolhardiness I knew all too well, was already set to run.

Holmes held us back all in check.

"No, I think not. Do not run. Do you hear that metallic, clinking sound? The beast is most certainly and securely chained, so it can not get to us, as yet. However, it blocks the doorway into the Witch's personal chambers quite effectively, so we can not get inside without passing it. To try now, would not be wise. We seem to be at an impasse," Holmes told us grimly, "at least for the moment."

"I think Mr. Holmes is correct," The Professor stated.

"And we must get into the Witch's chambers before she comes back, Mr. Holmes," Dorothy told us in haste. "We must get to her crystal globe, and there is also that magical mirror, and a special whistle, as well as the Golden Cap, she uses to control her winged monkeys. We must take all these magical contrivances away from her. Then we must set the Lion free."

"Right you are!" Holmes replied, realizing the importance of these various magical devices here in Oz, and that it may all have some connection to his case of the red poppy menace. "We will find a way inside, and we shall free your Lion friend also."

I put my faith in my friend and looked to him for an answer to our problem.

Sherlock Holmes looked around us quickly examining the hallway just in front of the door to the Witch's rooms. There was nothing to see there, at least nothing visible. I wondered what he was looking for. What did he see? There was nothing to see at all!

Finally Holmes gaze set upon our Scarecrow friend and his manner appeared most curious as he said to him confidentially in a low tone, "I am somewhat loath to ask this of you, my friend, but we are in dire need of your assistance and time is short."

The Scarecrow nodded and even gave Holmes a thin knowing smile. He was a sharp one, that Scarecrow, and I believe he knew just what was in my friend's mind.

"Ask away, what you must," he said simply.

"Well, could you spare us each two large handfuls of your straw stuffing?" Holmes asked him softly.

"Yes, and I think I know what you intend to do with it, Mr. Holmes. However, you know it will deplete me to... almost nothingness," the brave Scarecrow told my friend.

"I assure you, we shall retrieve every bit of straw and hay and stuff it back into your body if we are successful in my plan," Holmes promised him. Then he added grimly, "However, if we are not successful, then it matters little what we do afterwards, you must know that as well."

"Yes, I see. I can accept the risk. I think your idea may work. Go ahead, Mr. Holmes. Here! Take whatever you need of my straw."

Holmes nodded, commanded us quickly, "Come now, all of you, take two big hands full of the Scarecrow's straw. Then when I give the word we will all throw it at the end of the corridor over the head of the invisible hound. The straw should cover the hound and outline the form of the creature to us, at least making it's form visible to us. Then quickly using the Winkie's blades the Professor and I can have a go at it and kill it. Watson, take careful aim for the heart of the monster with your revolver and try to bring it down. Woodman, see to it you use your ax most effectively. Are you all ready?"

"Right you are, Holmes!" I stated, my hands now full of the Scarecrow's straw and awaiting his command to throw it upon the creature down the hallway. As far as where to aim my weapon at the creature's heart, I had no real idea where that might be located, but I decided to worry about that when I could actually see the creature—or at least see an outline of it to better judge my shots.

"At my command, everyone throw your straw high into the air at that end of the hallway, aim for the area directly over the creature by the doorway in front of the Witch's apartment," Holmes told us. Then he motioned us still closer to the beast and now the creature growled in dire warning. When Holmes had taken us as close as he dared, he then issued a loud command and ordered, "Now! Throw your straw!"

Then Holmes and I, Professor Wonder, Dorothy and the Tin Woodman let loose into the air with handfuls of the Scarecrow's straw and hay. It was a veritable barrage. The stuff flew into the air above the invisible beast, then floated gently down upon it. Gradually we saw that a form was taking shape before our eyes from the straw as it landed upon the beast.

Meanwhile, the poor Scarecrow lay flat upon the floor behind us at the other end of the corridor, empty of straw and hay, fully depleted and awaiting the success or failure of Holmes' plan..

The barrage of straw had worked well, it had flown into the air and slowly but surely flowed downward to land upon the invisible hound. Much of it fell upon the hound, and slowly but surely it created for us an outline of the creature that made it now visible to us.

Immediately Dorothy, Holmes, the Professor and I threw the Winkie blades at the creature, even as I withdrew my revolver, while the Tin Woodman attacked it with his ax. We were thankful the beast was still chained to the wall outside the Witch's chambers—though it strained and fought to escape and get at us. I knew we did not have a lot of time before it would shake itself loose from its restraints—or be released by the Witch—and be upon us. I feared the Witch herself might set it loose upon us at any moment. We had to work fast.

I aimed my revolver carefully and quickly got off four shots at a place in the beast where I assumed the heart of the giant hound might be located—it was merely a guess at that point as I followed the straw outline of the beast—but I must have guessed well as the gigantic creature yelped loudly and cried out in pain and then suddenly fell down motionless. I now could make out that the beast was truly enormous, and we were lucky that it had been chained, but now it was dead—or so I hoped.

"Is it dead, Watson?" Holmes asked me carefully.

I moved in closer and did a quick examination, there was no breathing, no heart beat. "Yes, it is dead. Most assuredly dead."

"Good, now quickly, we must scrape up every last bit of straw and hay and return it to poor Scarecrow right away," Dorothy told us in an urgent voice.

We immediately did as she asked and soon, sufficiently re-stuffed with his straw and hay filling his form once again, our Scarecrow friend was back to normal.

"That is much better!" the Scarecrow informed us with a wide grin.

"How do you feel?" I asked him.

"Never felt better," the Scarecrow told us, giving me a winning smile as he rearranged the straw in his clothing to make himself more comfortable.

"Now, let us carefully navigate the body of this dead hound that has barred us from entering the private chambers of the wicked Witch and go on inside," Holmes ordered our little group, "now that all of us are back together again."

We trod carefully, but quickly and soon opened the unlocked door—the evil Witch had no need of any lock to her chambers with such a formidable creature guarding her doorway and all her magical powers—and we were soon inside her private chambers.

Of course, the wicked Witch was there waiting for us!

CHAPTER 16: THE WITCH'S TRAP

The wicked Witch of the West was waiting for us in her chambers with about two dozen of her Winkie soldiers, who being enslaved by her sorcery, always did her bidding without any questions asked.

The ancient crone was a sickly pasty pallor that looked like dull colorless death, and as if to accent that feature of her face and skin, she was dressed in long black funeral weeds and wore a tall pointed black hat. It reminded me of the two hats that I had seen Holmes mention with such interest when we had been in Professor Wonder's home back in Kansas.

The Witch also carried a closed long black umbrella which she kept close to her person at all times. However, the most horrifying aspect of the Witch's physical appearance was her single horrid telescopic eye, that seemed to move inwards and outwards, forwards and backwards, like some ghastly flesh and blood telescope that was constantly focusing, examining, looking for what I could not ever know. It was eerie, and freakish.

I realized that the Witch had set a very nice trap for us, in the event we escaped her large invisible canine guardian, and now we had fallen right into her grasp.

"Welcome my young lady! And your unlucky friends too! So you killed my invisible hound, and made your way into my chambers after all! I see Mr. Sherlock Holmes, you did not heed my warning, a decision you shall soon regret! You think you passed my test? Well you shall not escape me this time!" Then the Witch screamed out an order in terrible rage to her minions, *"Go get them! Leave the girl for me!"*

Then the Winkies were fully upon us before we realized it, and in an instant a battle royal ensued as Holmes and I, and Professor Wonder, with Dorothy and her two brave companions fought the nasty beastly men that came at us from all directions, including terrifying overhead diving attacks off the top balcony, and head-on running charges. They thrust and slashed at us in an unmistakable attempt to cause us considerable serious wounds. They were not trying to capture us. It took only a moment to realize they were trying to kill us. We did not ask for quarter and it did not matter here now, but we fought back against them most desperately.

Our little group of companions fought back well against the attackers, however we had no choice, for we found ourselves in a fight for our very lives now. In a sidelong glance, I noticed the Witch laughing wildly with wicked joy as she urged her vile beast-men ever onward to attack us. She now screamed her orders boldly and clearly to her fiendish creatures to fall upon us, *"Kill them! Kill them all, but leave the girl for me!"*

Well, we found that we were indeed in a fight of our very lives. This would be a fight to the death. Now it was most clear to us that we either won this battle—or we were doomed. It was a grim realization. Nothing gathers your attention and clarity of purpose like the impending aspect of a bloody and violent death!

I quickly attempted to even the odds a bit. I took out my revolver, taking careful aim, then shot down five of the wicked little beasts stone dead. My shots were true and deadly, my former military training coming to the fore. That instantly evened up the odds significantly for us. At least for a moment. I saw the Tin Woodman strike down two more of the fiends with his mighty ax.

"Good work, Watson!" Holmes shouted out to me in encouragement as I saw him dispatch his own attacker, "and you, too, Woodman, good work!"

However, I felt our victory would prove short-lived indeed. I saw the Witch calling upon reinforcements, with more of the gruesome minions coming to aid her side in the battle.

"Stay alert, Watson! Watch yourself!" my friend replied, even as he fought off another attacker.

There was a tense moment of utter quiet, after which I saw that more of the Winkies were running into the huge high-ceilinged chamber through the front door that the huge hound had once guarded. They were also coming at us through a large open window from the outside—from somewhere. There were so many of them. I knew we had little time left to us if we were to win this fight, for the odds had now changed against us significantly.

I looked around me and noticed the Witch's crystal sphere that was held in a giant claw-like stand, and beside it there was a tall glass mirror that stood at least six feet in height. It was surely the magical mirror Dorothy had told us about.

"Holmes," I called out, pointing to these items as I fought off one of the Winkie soldiers that was trying to trap me in a corner. His knife made my fight most desperate. "Look! It is the Witch's crystal ball, and over there, near it—the magic mirror that Dorothy told us about!"

"I see them, Watson," Holmes responded to me quickly, for he was also deeply engaged in a battle with our attacking fiends. I noted he used a devastating combination of hard Japanese *karate* blows and *baritsu* kicks to knock out two attackers at once. "We must protect that mirror from any damage. Watson, come with me and let us form a protective barrier around it."

"You think it important?" I gasped, as I ran forward to join him.

"You want to get back home to London, do you not? Well, I believe that mirror is a portal between this world of Oz—and our own. So we may find it of some use."

"I see," I replied, watching the Witch fearfully as she begin to form up something with her hands. That was bad. It seems she could form bolts of lightning with her hands and use them as deadly weapons. There was no one here now to save us from the evil Witch's lightning bolts. It could prove a most deadly danger to us all.

"Holmes! The Witch!" I shouted in dire warning.

"Dorothy! Scarecrow, be careful!" Holmes shouted in warning to our companions and then he ducked down as a lightning bolt was shot like a rocket through the air at him and myself. That bolt missed us, thankfully. It almost hit Professor Wonder, who at that moment was heavily engaged fighting two adversaries, but he ducked just in time.

The bright yellow fire bolt missed us all thankfully, shooting just over our heads, and I felt considerable relief, but then my heart sank when I saw it crash upon the far wall. The fire started almost immediately, and soon it grew, and the Witch threw more bolts of lightning, one that hit the poor Scarecrow and set him to blazes. The straw man jumped about and cried out in sheer terror at the fire. Had not the Tin Woodman stepped in immediately to help him, the Scarecrow would have been in dire straights. Quickly the flames on the Scarecrow were put out by his brave companion and I was relieved to see that our friend was safe for the moment.

"Scarecrow, are you all right?" I shouted frantic, as I fought off another of the beastly attackers.

"Quite well now, thank you, Doctor," he replied as he soon rejoined the fight.

"You vile Witch! You almost killed poor Scarecrow!" Dorothy shouted in anger. Her little dog, Toto, backed up her feelings with a continuous stream of loud angry barks at the Witch.

Then the wicked Witch came at Dorothy from behind and tripped her with the curved handle of her umbrella. Dorothy fell to the floor—and suddenly one of her sliver shoes fell off her foot. Instantly the Witch grabbed up the precious shoe and placed it upon her own foot with a wicked laugh of victory.

"Now I have one of the silver shoes! Soon you will give me the other one, or die!" the Witch ordered the poor girl.

"No, you shall not have it! You tricked me, you tripped me with your umbrella! You must give me back my silver shoe, it is not yours, it is mine!" Dorothy ordered most forcefully. Good for her, I thought!

"I shall soon have both silver shoes and the magic that goes with them!" the Witch proclaimed confidently.

"Never!" Dorothy shouted defiantly.

The Witch just laughed and came at Dorothy in another wild attack upon the poor girl, and the two of them went at each other in a furious battle—each one trying to get the silver shoe off the foot of the other. The two fought madly, alone, as none of us could help Dorothy because of the attacks upon us by the relentless Winkies. So it was all up to Dorothy to win this battle on her own.

The Witch was furious with hate, but the girl was full of anger. Still and all, I noted that the Witch held back from any deadly or actual violent action upon my niece for the moment. I had heard that Dorothy had received the charm of the kiss of the Witch of the North upon her forehead and that it protected her from all harm—from the Witch and from her winged monkeys. The Witch knew this, so she could not hurt or kill Dorothy by normal or magical means in her effort to obtain that remaining shoe. Not until she had both of the silver shoes upon her feet would she have the power she craved—and then she would be able to kill Dorothy, and all of us as well.

Dorothy fought the Witch hard, doing her utmost to grab at the shoe on the Witch's foot, while the Witch tried to take the remaining shoe off Dorothy's foot. While the silver shoes held great power, their power only worked when worn by the same person who could call upon their magic. Dorothy moved around the Witch, grabbed at her, and pulled her down to the floor. They were in a wild fight for the magical shoes now, both rolling around on the floor in a furious battle.

"Give it to me!" the Witch demanded in a loud scream.

"No! They are mine!" Dorothy shouted back in anger.

Meanwhile another furious battle, this time with the Winkies, continued all around us. We had dispatched many of the Witch's minions, but more of the nasty brutes kept coming against us. I feared we were becoming overwhelmed, and none of us was in any position where we could help Dorothy at the moment and I knew I owed more than my life to the Woodman's ax.

"Unless we do something soon," I said to Holmes fearfully, "we may lose this battle, and our lives."

"Never fear, Watson," Holmes told me showing vivid confidence. "The game is afoot!"

"Well I hope so!" I replied gasping for breath in the heat of the fight, not quite sure what Holmes meant, but allowing a nervous hint of relief to enter my voice at my companion's words. I wondered just what his plan might be? I was sure he must have some plan. I told him bluntly, "Whatever we do, we must aid Dorothy."

"I am, Watson, I am."

Now I saw the wicked Witch busy working her hands to try to trip up Dorothy.

"Oh no you don't!" I heard my spunky niece blurt out in anger, for she saw what was to come from the Witch, and moved quickly to stop it.

"The Witch is going to hurt Dorothy, Holmes!" I blurted out in warning.

"I am aware of that, Watson," Holmes shouted back to me urgently. He was closest to Dorothy and I was sure he would move in straight away to help the girl—but instead he moved away.

He moved off!

"Holmes!" I shouted in alarm, "What are you doing?"

He did not answer me. He was the closest to Dorothy, the only one who could move in close enough to help her now. Instead of coming to her aid, I saw him quickly move away and suddenly pick up the Witch's umbrella, of all things. I wondered what he was about, but just then my attention was taken up by the Witch's continued attack to my niece. I looked over at her.

I heard Holmes quickly order Dorothy, "Pick up that bucket!"

It proved to be a bucket of water.

"No! No! Put that down!" The Witch barked out a furious command.

Dorothy had immediately taken up the large wooden bucket of water filled to the brim.

"No! No! Put that down now!" the Witch demanded, suddenly fearful. *"My umbrella! Where is my umbrella?"*

"Looking for this?" Holmes asked the Witch allowing a slim smile to play across his face, as he held the large closed black umbrella away from the Witch, so she could not reach it.

"My umbrella! Give it to me!" the Witch demanded in a horrid voice.

"I am afraid not," Sherlock Holmes replied simply.

"What!" the wicked Witch shrieked out in furious alarm.

"Now! Throw the water, Dorothy!" Holmes ordered my niece.

Then in one fell swoop Dorothy flung the contents of the large wooden bucket upon the Witch so that the water completely splashed over her and covered her body and all over her black clothing. The Witch was drenched. She was soaking wet now.

Then Dorothy took advantage of the confusion to take back her shoe off the Witch's foot, so that now she wore both of the magic silver shoes, and they were once again upon her feet where they belonged

"Good for you, Dorothy! Bravo!" I shouted, happy to see Dorothy get her shoes back, and to see the Witch get at least some comeuppance by being drenched with water, but at that time I had no real idea what Dorothy's action would truly mean to the Witch.

It was then that the most amazing thing happened.

The wicked Witch of the West looked at Holmes and myself in red furious anger, and then at Dorothy in undisguised fear and terror as she immediately began to scream in horrendous pain, for her body suddenly begin to deflate where the water had come into contact with her putrid flesh. Her single cyclopean eye wove and dodged like a burning snake. She continued to scream as thick smoke issued from her body, even as she seemed to bend down, diminishing in size, and then growing smaller and smaller, to become surrounded by a thick black cloud.

"My God, Holmes, what is happening? It is as if she is melting before our very eyes!" I stammered in awe. I realized we were watching the wicked Witch of the West shrink and deflate to nothingness as we watched incredulous. The Witch screamed out in rage and furious anger, as her form seemed to shrivel and dissolve from the water Dorothy had thrown upon her.

"I am ruined! All my lovely wickedness has been for naught! Curse you, Sherlock Holmes!" the Witch screamed her last words as she proceeded to extinguish herself, her form shrinking lower and lower down to the floor. She was melting away like brown sugar in a hot oven. I could see that soon the Witch would become just a flat wide puddle of thick brown sludge upon the floor.

"Holmes, how did you know about the water?" I asked astounded by what I had just seen.

"Well, it is quite elementary, through Professor Wonder's observation of never having seen rain in Oz, that made it peculiar for the Witch to be so obsessed with an umbrella. It can only have been for her fear of water," he told me simply.

Her Winkie slaves saw what had happened and now they all came towards us curiously, surrounding us, but in a moment their attack ended and soon all the Witch's vile minions were silent. I wondered what it all meant.

Then the leader of the Winkies came forward, looked at Dorothy, Holmes and myself, and asked carefully, "The Witch…she is dead?"

"Yes, the Witch is dead!" Holmes stated boldly.

There was silence for a long moment. What they call in dime novels, the pregnant pause. It was most daunting as I wondered what was to happen now.

"Then we are free of the wicked Witch and of her magic!" the Winkie leader proclaimed in unimagined joy, and all the Winkies cheered. Soon they left the chamber and were gone. It was not too long before our little group found ourselves alone.

"The Witch is… dead!" I blurted out in excited victory, but I soon learned I was a bit too precipitous in my judgment.

That is because before the Witch was fully gone and had entirely melted away, a tiny part of her remained, and I felt a pang of terror when I saw one of her arms rise out of the brown muck, and with her hand she flung one last glowing bolt of lightning that flew straight and true in the direction of Sherlock Holmes—but while my companion ducked and the bolt missed him—it hit the magical mirror instead. The mirror's glass shattered with a resounding roar and then fell to the floor in a million broken pieces.

"The mirror!" I cried out in warning, that changed to horror when I saw what happened to the magical device. "It is destroyed!"

"Yes, rather tragic for us I am afraid, Watson. However, the Witch is surely dead now," Holmes spoke up to our small group in a grim voice. "Dorothy and her friends have the victory they sought, even though the magic mirror used by the Witch to send the red poppies to our world has also been destroyed. It may have been our best bet to get back home, but it's destruction does stop the trade in the red poppy powder."

"Yes, I am afraid you may be right, Holmes, but now what?"

Sherlock Holmes gave me a wry look, "Well, with the mirror destroyed, there will be no more shipments of that deadly red poppy powder to our world. For I am now certain this is the pathway. However that magic mirror may have also offered us a way to get back home, and that is now closed off to us."

My face fell into a pall of gloom as I realized the truth of the Great Detective's words. I feared that Holmes and I were now trapped here in Oz for the rest of our lives. I hardly knew what to say about that terrible realization.

Dorothy, the Scarecrow, and the Tin Woodman came towards us. They had the victory they had fought so hard for. The wicked Witch was dead. They soon freed their friend, the cowardly Lion, from his cell in the dungeon, and all were together again. It was a happy time for them. A happy reunion. Not so for Holmes and I, nor the Professor, for we each wanted to get back home—not to mention poor Dorothy.

It was at that dark moment that the Witch's magical crystal ball suddenly came to life. We noticed a cloudy vision appearing within the crystal that caused us all to form around the mysterious orb and look deeply into it, and the image that was forming within the magical crystal globe.

"What is it, Mr. Holmes?" Dorothy asked most curious, as Holmes and I, with my niece and her companions stood expectantly around the crystal ball and looked into it intently.

"Someone is using another crystal ball, to contact us, much as my Miranda did," the Professor explained as we all watched the globe in fascination.

What was it that was forming upon the face of the crystal?

"It is coming to life!" I whispered in awe, for I also had seen such a magical device in use in Professor Wonder's home back in Kansas. It was both surreal and ethereal.

All of us stood around the Witch's globe of magical round crystal trying to make out what was taking shape there through the fog and mist that we saw within it. Soon we could see that the image forming there appeared to be the face of a man, and it was the face of a man that I was sure Holmes knew quite well. He was older now, but it was the same man I recognized from some years back, a man who was supposed to be dead.

The man was well dressed in fashionable modern London garb, his small cruel eyes were sharp and bright, his lips parched in grim anticipation. He was incredibly angry.

"Sherlock Holmes!" the man cried out in ill-concealed rage.

"Moriarity!" Holmes growled back heatedly. "So, I surmised as much but could attain no proof. The Red Poppy Menace outbreak in London surely had the taint of your vile involvement, so news of your demise was greatly exaggerated. You are alive!"

"Yes, I am alive, no thanks to you! I am alive and have been in hiding for some time. And you survived the Reichenbach trap I set for you rather well," the man in the globe replied grimly, hatred oozing out of each one of his words. "I though it best for me to lay undercover these few years, operating even deeper in the shadows as you can now see. It was better for the world to suppose that I was dead, as it was for you to have the world suppose that you were dead, as well. In your case, too bad your death was not a fact."

"I feel the same way about you. So, I see that you are involved with this Red Poppy Menace," Holmes spoke firmly, annoyance creeping into his voice.

"Yes, and I am sure you know that I have been watching all that has taken place there in the castle through the wonders of my own crystal globe," the criminal genius from London told us with a haughty leer. "I may be unable to interfere there, but I now have full knowledge of all that has transpired there in that room."

Holmes allowed a grim smile for he had assumed much of this all along, "I had an inkling that only a snake such as yourself could be behind such a scheme as the Red Poppy Menace. You contacted the Witch here through the crystal globe and arranged with her to have her minions harvest the deadly red poppy for you, and brought to you by her creature, Songa, the brother of the late and unlamented Tonga—a banished evil Munchkin whose twisted mind made him the first user of the powder. The Witch had Songa bring the powder to you in London through the use of her magical mirror—and your own—for you must have a counterpart in London."

"You are, as usual, quite astute, Mr. Holmes," Moriarty said allowing a vile sneer of pure hatred to cloud his face. "I see you have dispatched my most useful ally, the Witch. She is dead?"

"She is most assuredly dead, just as is her sister," Holmes told the man whose face was shown to us in the crystal sphere. I was shocked for I had no doubt that Moriarty was still alive now, nor that he also had a crystal glass orb in his possession in London—as well as a magical mirror—which is how he was able to make contact between our world and Oz. It was utterly fantastic, but true, and I feared what was to come of us now. Dorothy and her companions looked on in awe and wonder at what was transpiring before them, but for the moment they said not a word.

Moriarty spit out in venomous anger, "Yes, the drug made from the red poppy would have made me quite wealthy and powerful. It would enable me to form an army of slaves to the drug, slaves who would do my every bidding, but you have once again interfered with my plans and now wrecked everything I have secretly worked so hard to achieve over these last few years in Oz."

"Think nothing of it. It is my pleasure, Professor Moriarty," Holmes stated sharply, this time allowing his pride to show boldly for one triumphant moment. "Any time I can derail one of your nefarious schemes I am always ready and willing to do so. No matter what the cost."

"Well it shall cost you dearly, this time, I am afraid, Mr. Holmes," Moriarty threatened with a twisted grimace.

"We shall see," Holmes replied, not intimidated at all by his mere threats.

Moriarty's face showed a hint of intense anger and rage, but he soon masterfully took control of himself and a most evil leer looked out at us from the glass ball, and then an ominous deadly smile came to his face as he spoke boldly to Holmes, "Yes, you have been successful this time, but it shall be the last time for you, Mr. Sherlock Holmes. For with the Witch's magic mirror destroyed, you and your companion, Doctor Watson, have no way to get back home to our world. To London. I am afraid Sherlock Holmes, that you are now trapped in Oz forever. Amazingly, you are the only one who knows I am alive and now I am assured my secret is safe with you! You know my secret but you can do nothing about it—I am still dead as far as the world knows. My knowing that fact is almost worth all the trouble you have put me through. To know you will never be able to get back to our world, or interfere with my plans ever again, gives me much comfort! Enjoy your stay in Oz, Mr. Holmes. I shall just have to content myself with expanding my powers here in London, and eventually throughout the British Empire, and then the entire world. With you gone, nothing can stop me now!"

"Moriarty!" Holmes shouted in a voice that was part anger, part a promise of stark revenge. I do not believe I ever saw my friend so distressed. The realization of the news that my companion's greatest enemy was in fact, still alive, shocked me to the core. The fact that Moriarty was involved in this Oz poppy business, shook me to the very foundations of my being. On top of all that, it now seemed impossible for us to ever get back home again to London to alert Lestrade. It was a horrible realization, inconceivable.

Then the crystal ball went blank, to become just clear crystal glass and the image of Moriarty's face was gone.

No one said a word for a long moment.

"Well, that was quite enlightening," Holmes said in a lighter voice. He had already recovered his composure.

"Holmes, why did you not tell me that monster Moriarty was still alive?" I asked, surprised by what had happened, and upset by finding out this knowledge now.

"Good, Watson, I am sorry, but I had no conclusive proof that Moriarty was indeed alive, so I did not want to alarm you unnecessarily. He had gone deep undercover after the events at Reichenbach, and kept clean of crime for some time. I see now that he was working on this red poppy scheme here in Oz."

"Incredible, Holmes! He is your greatest enemy, a deadly viper, and now he is living free in London, while we are to be stranded here in Oz forever," I stated grimly.

Holmes looked at me carefully, "While we may have a problem getting back home, Watson, we will get home!"

That seemed starkly untrue now. My head was swirling with all kinds of terrible thoughts about all that I had just learned. Then I looked over at my friend and smiled with all the reassurance I could muster, "If there is some way to get us home, I know that you will find that way, Holmes."

Sherlock Holmes offered me a grim scowl and I could see the doubt in his face had grown, "Watson, you may be placing too much emphasis upon my powers. However, there is another avenue of action that comes to me. We came here by hot air balloon with Frank Baum, his brother Oscar Baum also came here by balloon, so who is to say that we can not get back home the same way?"

I nodded, curious but not certain of the outcome of his words. It seemed most sketchy at best. Still and all, Holmes' words gave me some hope. Which was essential for us all. Were we, in truth, defeated? Were Holmes and I to remain trapped here in Oz, forever? It was a bitter thought. Or was there still a way for us to get back home to London? I was not sure. Flying here through a thunderous cyclone of which now there are none, in a rickety hot air balloon had somehow worked to get us here, but how would we fly home in such a thing? Did we need another storm to propel us home in the same balloon? And what direction would we travel to get back home? I was stumped and not sure about much at that point concerning our future.

I looked over at Sherlock Holmes and saw him in deep thought. What was to become of us now? And then there was my niece, Dorothy. Poor child. Was there a way for her to get back home to Kansas? After all, we had come here to rescue her and bring her back home. That had been the very reason for our mission here in the first place, though now I knew that Holmes had had another motive for coming here to Oz. A more concealed one, that being the Red Poppy Menace. Perhaps even some suspicions about Moriarty and his involvement in it? Regardless, in any case, we had achieved the first part of our mission, but what of the rest of it? I dared to put the question to my companion on how we would get back home to London, and what was to become of Dorothy?

"I am sure we can work this out somehow, Watson. In any case we must return to the City of Emeralds. Perhaps we can find the answers we need there?" Holmes told me, and then with Professor Wonder, Dorothy and her three companions—the large cowardly Lion had also joined us freed from his cell in the castle dungeon by the Scarecrow—I knew we must begin the arduous trek back to the wondrous city that was the home of the Wizard of Oz.

That was when Dorothy spoke up telling us, "Mr. Holmes, Uncle John, Professor Wonder, we need not trek back to the city on foot. I can use the Golden Cap, it is a magical headpiece that has the most amazing glittering black pearl on top that was used by the Witch to command the winged monkeys. The person who is in possession of the Golden Cap gets three wishes to command the monkeys. I can use one wish to call upon the king of the winged monkeys and order them to fly us all back to the Wizard's city."

And that is exactly what we did.

CHAPTER 17: THE WIZARD OF OZ

The Good Witch of the North and the gatekeeper greeted us at the gateway to the City of Emeralds. We were joined by a large crowd of cheering citizens who all appeared most joyful at our return and upon hearing the good news of our victory over the wicked Witch of the West. The wicked Witch who was no more! The wicked Witch who was now very dead!

They met Holmes and myself, along with Professor Wonder, Dorothy and her three companions, with a large elegant victory parade where we were led as honored guests throughout the city to the Wizard's magnificent palace.

The people all wildly cheered us as we passed them on the elegant avenues and byways of the great city. It was a wonderful parade throughout the fabulous city. It was a most honored return for us to this lovely city, and the people cheered us happily, many calling out Dorothy's name in ringing praise. My great niece and I were warmed by the affection of the people of Oz for her, and for each one of us who had been involved in the defeat of the wicked Witch. Even Holmes was not unaffected by this regal treatment and joyful recognition of our accomplishment. Little Toto just barked in excitement and joy, and then snuggled close to Dorothy.

Professor Wonder was eager to see his brother after so many years and rushed us towards the palace in great haste.

"We have returned from our mission, Holmes, and the wicked Witch is dead and Dorothy is free," I told my friend as we walked through the cheering throngs that lined the streets and wide avenues of the great city. It was a moment of sheer happiness that we each savored.

"Yes, Watson, we have accomplished much, much more in fact than I ever anticipated when we first embarked upon this most strange adventure," Holmes told me in a soft, thoughtful tone. "We also put an end to Moriarty's partnership with the Witch and their harvesting of the dread red poppy powder, and their transportation of it through the magical mirrors to London, where it would be used to enslave our people."

"Yes, Holmes, a most dastardly plan there for sure, but it is ended now with the magic mirror here broken, even though it has shattered our swift return home," I added grimly.

"We shall see, Watson, we shall see," Holmes spoke up in a firm voice that gave me some hope, but he would say no more upon the matter, and I wondered if he was just being upbeat for my benefit. Or did he know something that I did not?

"Well, it is truly a sad turn of events for us," I said softly, "for I do not see another way."

"Perhaps that other way, is by the manner that we came here? By hot air balloon?" Holmes told me with a sly grin, "or perhaps not?"

I simply shook my head at that, my friend was being his usual enigmatic self once again. I could not see how we could ever use a hot air balloon to get back home—even though we had come to Oz in just such a manner. After all, it had been during a terrible storm, and there were no such storms here. What power could we use to propel a balloon back home. Magic? How would that work? I had no idea. We had no route or plan of travel. It seemed preposterous. I was perplexed by the dilemma and it made me sad, even as I voiced these concerns to my friends.

Holmes did not seem to despair of any of these facts, nor did he comment upon my musings at the moment. I did not know what else to say upon the matter, but I suspected he was comensorating upon some course of action. At least I hoped so.

Holmes saw my distress and gave me a wan smile and I immediately cheered up, for in that moment I knew that Sherlock Holmes had not given up at all, and that knowledge buoyed my spirits immensely. I knew he would find a way out of this problem for us. Perhaps, in a magical land— where magic truly worked—anything might indeed be possible? I wondered if magic might be the answer to our problem.

"In any case, our being stranded here may be well worth it, Holmes, if we have truly put a stop to Moriarty's plans."

Holmes merely nodded, I could see he was thinking through the problem with that marvelous mind of his.

"What do you think, Holmes?" I asked my friend impatiently.

"I think that we shall work it through, Watson, and we shall find some way back home—if it exists. In fact, I am sure that one does. The way we came here could be the answer for us to go back home. Perhaps. I tell you this in all candor, I have not read Challenger's book for naught, nor for mere entertainment. In his book he tells of a most interesting phenomena. He proposes all cyclones are not alike—like the hands of a clock, they can be tuned forward, but also reset backwards! If we can find a massive cyclone that revolves backwards, such a storm might well be our answer to get home. I am readying to talk this through with the Professor and see if he agrees. So if a forward cyclone brought us here, why not a backwards one, to bring us home?"

"But by hot air balloon?" I asked quite dubious, and showing it. "Without a massive storm to furnish the power to propel it, I can not see it taking us very far. And in a backwards storm? Where do we find such a storm? Is such a storm even possible? Do they exist? Regardless, in another storm any balloon would be destroyed, I fear, and us along with it."

"Cheer up, both of you," Professor Wonder told us with a big smile. "I have found my brother, Oscar—the Wizard. I have heard he was placed under a spell by the wicked Witch and held a prisoner by her minion, some evil twisted Munchkin named Songa."

I looked towards my detective friend, "Songa?"

"The Good Witch told us of this Songa, the younger brother of Tonga, and he was the beastlike fellow who was following me in London. The Witch must have ordered him back here to Oz, to abduct the Wizard."

"Indeed, that is exactly what happened! Once the Witch was killed, her power and her spell was broken, her minion ran away, and my brother, Oscar, is now free. The Witch's creature was captured and is now cooling his heels in the city jail. And now I am happy that I have found my brother and he is hale and hearty. I am sure he will find a way to help you two gentlemen. And if not, I will do all I can to help you," the Professor explained in a bright manner.

I nodded, that seemed quite cricket of him.

"And what of me?" Dorothy asked the Professor, she stood near us with her three patient companions.

Professor Wonder looked grim and did not reply.

"I do not want to remain in Oz, or the City of Emeralds, as nice as it might be. I want to return to my home. To Kansas. I am worried about Aunt Em and Uncle Henry. The storm may have hurt them. They may need me. I must return home."

The Professor said, "Let us see what the Wizard says upon that matter."

* * * *

It was not long before the grand parade finally reached the Wizard's Great Palace.

Professor Wonder and the Good Witch escorted our small group into the massive building and into the huge audience chamber of the magnificent Wizard of Oz.

Inside the immense audience chamber there was a great curtain that covered the full wall at the far end of the massive room. Holmes and I, along with Dorothy and Toto, and the Scarecrow, the Tin Woodman, and a shivering Lion, now stood before the large curtain patiently waiting.

Professor Wonder and the Good Witch stood with us, as the Professor called out in a rather humorous voice, "Oh, Oz, the Great and Terrible? We are here at your command!"

Suddenly we were assailed by loud noises and great gusts of wind and white smoke that burst out from behind the large curtain. Then appearing upon the surface of the great curtain we saw a stark wizardly face. It was a big head wearing a turban with a great jewel in the center of it, and he appeared most stern and even scary. The Lion seemed to wilt at the very sight of him. I grew concerned, for this was certainly not the type of greeting I had expected.

Then a loud and powerful voice spoke up most threateningly, "Who dares enter the audience chamber of the Great and Terrible Wizard of Oz!"

There was a long fearful moment of silence.

I did not know how to respond, and Holmes remained strangely silent, and then he burst out with the most wild laughter! I had never seen my friend show so much mirth and amusement.

Professor Wonder then spoke up loudly in a caustic and rather annoyed voice, "Oh, come off it now, Oscar! It is I, your brother, Frank, and you know it! Where are you?"

There was a rather long nervous silence.

Then the Professor's voice changed to a more friendly manner as if this were all some kind of inside joke among the two brothers. Which, in fact, it proved to be.

The Professor spoke up briskly, "I see you are still playing at that Wizard humbug! Come off it now, Oscar! It is I, Frank, come here and meet us."

"Oh, I am so sorry, brother," the voice of the Wizard now spoke in a normal tone with a light laugh and then a man suddenly stepped out from behind the large curtain. He was a youngish gentleman, rather distinguished in a scholarly sort of way, with a kind and mild appearance. He had dark hair and a thick dark moustache. I now realized why he used the scare tactics he had employed as Wizard, for his physical appearance was not intimidating in the least, and in a world full of witches and other nasty fiends, that appearance did not instill any confidence or fear.

The Wizard smiled a wide grin at the sight of his brother, and the two embraced and reminisced and laughed just as they must have done when they were youngsters back in Omaha."

"Ever the showman, eh Oscar?" the Professor gently chided his brother, and then I saw that the man who was the Wizard of Oz was almost the spitting image of Professor Wonder. He told us confidentially, "When Oscar and I were children we used to play a game that we were mighty Wizards. We even dressed up as magicians with tall pointy hats and long magical robes."

"It was great fun, was it not, Frank?" the Wizard asked his brother.

"Oh, yes, those certainly were the days!" L. Frank Baum answered with a wide grin of fond remembrance.

"So they really are brothers?" I spoke softly to Holmes.

"Yes, twins in fact, Watson. I noted the fact long ago when we were guests in Professor Wonder's home back in Kansas. Recall the two wizard hats? The photos of the two boys? Twins. Their similar attire in the photo. As boys in their youth they played magicians in a stage act at the state fair."

"That is true, Mr. Holmes," Professor Wonder told us with a wide grin, "We were the Baum Brothers, magicians *par excellence!*"

Then Oscar Baum, the Wizard of Oz—whose initials of his first two names I recalled were 'O' and 'Z' creating the acronym 'OZ', now came over to meet us in joyful happiness.

"Welcome all of you to the City of Emeralds and to Magical Oz, as I have christened it," the Wizard told us in enthusiastic greeting, shaking all our hands most warmly, and hugging his brother, Frank, with great warmth once more. It was obvious the brothers were overjoyed to see each other again after so long a parting. "I am so happy to see you, Frank. And you others as well! And Dorothy, little Dorothy! I see that you are safe and free of the wicked Witch!"

"Thanks to the Scarecrow, the Tin Woodman, and the Lion," Dorothy spoke up and her three companions all stood a little bit taller at her words of praise and they each smiled deeply. She then looked at us and continued, "As well as Mr. Holmes here, and of course, my great Uncle, John—Doctor Watson."

"Then all is good," Oscar the Wizard spoke up and everyone cheered. "All is good and well in Oz now!"

"What about our wishes? You promised if we brought proof of the Witch's death you would grant our wishes?" the Scarecrow asked firmly now. "The Witch is dead."

"Just so, just so," the Wizard finally told them all with a smile. "It shall be done!"

* * * *

The Wizard proved as good as his word.

"Dorothy, you shall be first. You want to return to Kansas, do you not?" the Wizard asked her with a smile.

"Yes, sir, please!" she replied clapping her hands in joy that her wish was going to be fulfilled after so long a time.

"Glinda, would you like to do the honors?" the Wizard asked the golden haired beautiful witch. This was the younger sister of the Witch of the North, who was also a Witch in Oz.

Glinda, the Good Witch of the South smiled lovingly and said, "Dear Dorothy, your way home was always been within your grasp. See the silver shoes you wear upon your feet? The silver shoes worn by the wicked Witch of the East, whom you most definitely killed—and whose shoes you wear hold a powerful charm. Well, just as their power worked for you when you threw the bucket of water upon her sister—I am sure you can use the shoes to take you any place you like in Oz, even back home. All you need do is click their heels together and say that you want to go home to Kansas, and you shall be transported back there instantly and safely. Such is the power of the good magic of Oz."

"Oh, my, I don't know what to say! Thank you, so very much!" Dorothy cried out in joy. Then she looked toward her three companions and a sad smile crossed her face. "Oh, Scarecrow, Tin Woodman, and Lion, I am going to miss you all so very much."

"We will miss you too, Dorothy," the Scarecrow spoke up for the three companions. The other two being much to overcome by emotion to speak. The Tin Woodman feared to cry as he might rust, but the Lion carefully took the oil can and oiled his metallic joints before his tears caused any rust to form upon him.

There were hugs and more tears as they said their fond goodbyes.

"Fear not, Dorothy, I shall take care of your friend's needs," the Wizard told her with a warm smile. "So you may leave Oz knowing they will be well taken care of."

"Oh, thank you, you really are a great and wonderful Wizard!" Dorothy spoke up joyfully.

The Wizard seemed to glow at the praise.

That done, goodbyes were spoken once more. The hugs and kisses flowed.

I said my goodbye to my great niece Dorothy, telling her I was so proud of the young lady she had become and asked her to write me in London so we could exchange letters. She agreed to do so. I am sure we would each have much to write upon concerning our various adventures in the magical land of Oz.

Then Dorothy clicked the heels of her silver shoes together one time and she said, "Take me back home to Kansas and my Aunt Em"—and then the silver shoes gave off a puff of white smoke and apparently did their work—*but they did not!*

Nothing happened.

Dorothy had not moved, she was still standing there plain as could be.

"Try it again," Glinda asked with curious concern.

My niece clicked the heels of her silver shoes together once more but nothing happened.

"I do not understand," Glinda said astonished.

"Most strange," the Wizard added in a curious voice.

"That should not happen, the magic of the shoes should work," the Professor stated with obvious surprise.

"Yes, it should," Ginda added quite surprised.

Dorothy began to cry, "The magic of the shoes is not working! I will be stranded here in Oz forever!"

I looked towards Holmes, "What is happening?"

Holmes nodded, looked over at Glinda the Good Witch, "If I am not much mistaken, the magic of the shoes may only work here in Oz, and can not be used to take Dorothy home to Kansas, in our world."

Glinda nodded thoughtfully, "Of course, you must be correct, Mr. Holmes. Magic can sometimes be very tricky and this is a request that I have never before made for anyone to leave Oz."

"Well what does Dorothy do now?" I asked crestfallen for the poor child.

"I do not know how to get home," Dorothy spoke tearfully to the Wizard.

"Yes, Kansas. That is quite a long distance away form Oz," the Wizard stated with a wise nod of his head and a twitch of his bushy eyebrows. He shook his head sadly.

"You must help Dorothy," the Scarecrow spoke up in a pleading voice.

"Yes, please help Dorothy get back home," the Tin Woodman added.

"Dorothy needs your help, please, Oh Wizard," the Lion said, then he added a loud roar to accent his words. His voice certainly sounded ferocious.

"Yes indeed, I shall help her," the Wizard replied with a sure nod of his head but then said no more.

I feared old Oscar was giving us all another humbug and looked at him carefully, but Holmes caught my eye and implored me to keep mum for the moment. I decided to comply with his wishes, for now.

"And when you help me, you must also help my three companions here with their requests," Dorothy added, pointing to the Scarecrow, the Tin Woodman and the Lion.

"Mr. Wizard, sir," the Scarecrow continued respectfully, "I also speak for myself and my two companions here. We need your help with the personal matters Dorothy mentioned—your previous promise for an intellect for me, a heart for my Tin Woodman friend here, and acknowledgement of his acts of bravery for this wonderful courageous Lion. You promised us these gifts weeks ago if we helped Dorothy kill the wicked Witch of the West, and now the Witch is most assuredly dead."

The Wizard nodded thoughtfully, admitting his promise to the trio.

The Tin Woodman and the Lion each smiled eagerly, awaiting the great man's response.

CHAPTER 18: HOME TO LONDON

I cleared my throat to get everyone's attention.

"Ah, yes, and you too, Doctor Watson," Professor Wonder spoke up now. "Watson and Holmes have a dire need to get back home to London. I wish I had a way that can be easily accomplished."

Then the Wizard looked over to Holmes and myself, "And you two gentlemen, who are most decidedly here being out of your time and world. I am afraid I am at a loss as to how you can return to Kansas?"

Holmes looked from the Wizard to his brother, the Professor.

"Professor, we need *you* to take us back home to London," Holmes spoke up firmly, addressing the Wizard's brother.

Professor Wonder—Frank Baum—then replied with a gentle smile, "Oh, no, Oscar—oh Great Wizard, my brother. I had planned to stay here with him, but if need be I shall take you two gentlemen back home to London."

"And how is that possible, any how?" I asked. Even his brother the Wizard, looked at Holmes wanting to hear the explanation on this great boon he was going to bestow upon us. I could not see how Frank Baum would be able to guide us back to London, of all places. I awaited an explanation.

"By use of the Professor's balloon," Holmes said quite confidently now. "He is the only one who can transport us back to London. I have some reverse cyclone theory from Challenger's text that just might point us directly to London."

"So if that is how it must be, I shall do it," said the Professor with a winning smile. "I believe with Holmes' help I can find a way to take us back home in my hot air balloon, and the little lady too, if she would like to come with us."

"But how?" I blurted, looking over at Holmes, as I thanked Frank Baum—Professor Wonder—and shook his hand heartily. Holmes had been correct all along!

Sherlock Holmes told me, "I had our little friends, the Munchkins—or my Oz Irregulars—charming little fellows—bring the hot air balloon here to the City of Emeralds when you, the Wizard, were under the power of the wicked Witch. Frank's balloon, unlike Oscar's, has some special qualities that enhance it's powers. I had the Tinsmiths do some work upon it, providing a guide, and I can show the Professor how to reset the controls and directional indicators to Challenger's specifications so that the balloon will take us back home, to our world, directly to London, England."

The Professor, Frank Baum smiled, "I have very precise controls, Doctor Watson, so do not fear. I can even set our landing in a most pleasant pasture that is inside Hyde Park. Will that be sufficient for you?"

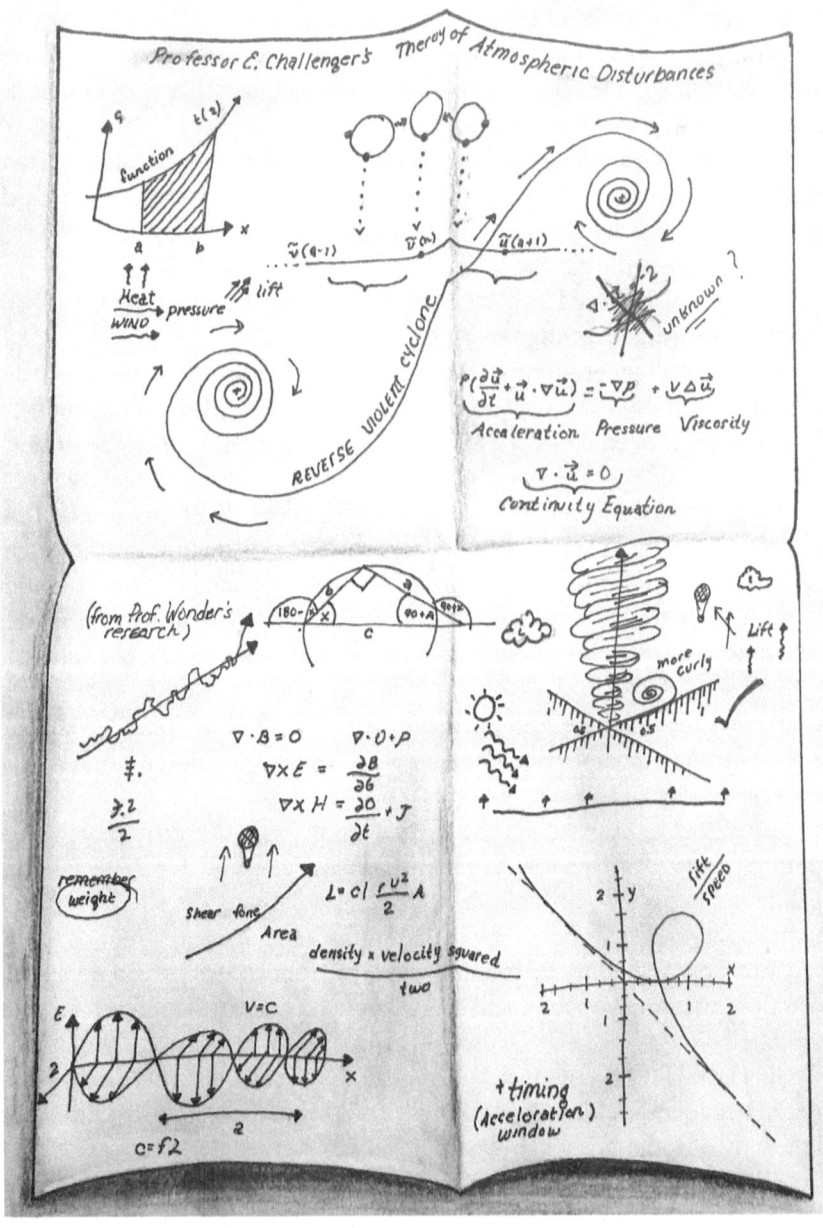

"Quite sufficient, and I thank you," I replied in a better mood now.

"I also offer you my gratitude, Mr. Baum," Holmes added with obvious sympathy. "I am sorry to take you from your brother, Oscar. I am sure that my study of the weather patterns charted by Professor Challenger, will enable us to use a cyclone that has a reverse rotation to take us back home to London. We should be able to find one for our needs once we are up in the higher atmosphere."

L. Frank Baum smiled warmly, "Yes, that should work. Now, I must thank you both, for without you and Watson, and our journey here to Oz, I would never have been able to see my dear brother, Oscar. I have missed him these many years. Also, Dorothy and my brother, Oscar, would never have been saved from the evil plans of the wicked Witch without you and Watson, Mr. Holmes. Now Dorothy can return home to Kansas where she belongs, and her three friends will have their requests met—and I can return you and Watson safely back home to London. I am sure your return will certainly surprise that Moriarty fellow you seem to be so much concerned about."

Then Oscar, in a booming Wizardly voice called forth the king of the Winkies, lately slaves of the wicked Witch, but newly freed and much redeemed in their nature.

The Winkie king bowed, then handed Frank Baum the Witch's crystal globe, saying, "I give you this so you may keep in contact with your brother in Oz, when you go home."

Frank Baum took the globe with great joy, and looked it over fondly. It reminded him of his late lamented Miranda. "Thank you! Thank you all! Now not all is lost! Now Oscar and I will have a way of communication, as well as a manner of warning should evil ever again return to Oz."

There were loud cheers and much happiness at this revelation.

I did not want to think just then about evil showing it's face once again in Oz, but now I knew the man Holmes called The Napoleon of Crime, Professor Moriarty, was still alive and in London! That knowledge was now incontrovertible and of great concern for Holmes and myself.

"It surely will surprise Moriarty, my friend," Sherlock Holmes told Frank Baum with a wide smile. "And now I must thank you—and the people of Oz and the City of Emeralds, one and all. Watson and I thank everyone and wish you well as we take our leave. And we will take Dorothy with us as well."

"She can come with us?" I asked happily.

"No problem, Watson, there is plenty of room in our balloon basket for one more passenger," Holmes told me, then he looked at Dorothy and asked her, "The speed and accommodations may not be what you expected, but would you like to come with us?"

"Would I! Of course, Mr. Holmes!" Dorothy shouted in sheer joy.

Sherlock Holmes and I smiled happily.

"Then it is all settled!" the Wizard said triumphantly.

"There is one more thing," Holmes spoke up firmly, but in a conciliatory tone. "This key. Here is the key, free your people, clarity is the best vision. The people here no longer need to wear their emerald-hued spectacles. And certainly not to have them locked on. Release them, and they will love you all the more for it."

"Of course, you are correct, Mr. Holmes, and it shall be done right away," Oscar Baum nodded, as Holmes gave him the key to unlock the green-hued spectacles of the people of the city.

Then Holmes, Dorothy, and I, with Frank Baum—entered the basket of Professor Wonders' marvelous balloon—and we helped him set the controls as he instructed us.

"Goodbye Mr. Holmes, and Dorothy, and you too Doctor Watson," the Wizard of Oz, Oscar Baum—who proved to be a rather gentle and decent humbug after all—called out to us. "And to you, Frank, my long lost brother, never forget me and the adventures you shared in this wonderful world."

"I shall never forget you, Oscar, nor Oz. I shall memorialize it all in my writings!"

Then once more assuming his Professor Wonder persona, Baum ordered Holmes to stoke up the flames of the fire to heat up the giant airbag, as we unlashed the balloon so it would rise into the atmosphere. Soon the bag began to fill and then lift gently upwards into the rarefied air of Oz. We waved and shouted more goodbye's and the crowd chanted sweet goodbyes back at us.

"Hold on tightly to that little dog, missy," Baum instructed Dorothy with a wide grin, "we may have a bumpy ride."

Then Holmes and I, and Dorothy, with Frank Baum, in the basket of our balloon floated gently upwards, ever upwards, over the City of Emeralds as all the inhabitants ran after us and cheered us along our route once more waving wildly. It was a bittersweet parting, for I had certainly taken a keen fancy to this most magical place and it's inhabitants. Oz! Imagine! Even the name was magical.

"Well, Holmes, what now?" I asked him with a sigh of relief tinged by a hint of sadness that our grand adventure had at last come to an end and our balloon was floating gently in the air.

"Yes, Watson, if Professor Challenger's equations are correct, soon we shall be back home in London. Then I have much work to do."

I nodded, surely knowing he was thinking about Moriarty. I put that thought out of my mind for the moment and looked around at the clear blue sky, now that we were up high into the atmosphere and well on our way home, I said simply, "Well, Holmes, we did it!"

"Yes we did, Watson, we certainly did."

Dorothy asked, "And what of me, Mr. Holmes?"

"You shall spend some time in London as our guest, and then we shall bring you and Mr. Baum to Liverpool and buy you first class tickets on a fast steamship to take you both to New York, and then back to Kansas."

"I will accompany you," Baum spoke up with a smile, "to be sure you return home safely."

"Thank you, Frank," I told Mr. Baum, happy that he would look out for my niece's safety on their journey home to America.

We traveled through the upper atmosphere for many hours. I do not know how we were able to navigate that balloon without a massive storm to furnish us with the power to propel our small sky ship, but Frank Baum assured me that the magic of Oz would work for us and take us home where we belonged. We did indeed find a cyclone storm and it had a reverse rotation, just what we needed according to Holmes—via his reading of Challenger's book—to take us home to London.

Holmes did not elaborate upon the process. I took it that any explanation would also include the magical powers of Oz, inexplicable and mysterious, so I held back on my many questions about the magic of Oz effecting our trip home. If it did at all. All my questions about magic remained unasked for the time being. I was just grateful we were on the way home. It must be as the Good Witch of the North had told us when we first met her in Munchkinland, that good magic is far stronger than evil magic in Oz. I looked at the Professor, who surely was a magician of some kind, and wondered about his own future.

"And now what of you?" I asked Mr. Baum, who had passed himself off as the former Professor Wonder, but I could now think of him only as Frank Baum. "What will you do now? Will you continue your act as The Marvelous Professor Wonder in America and continue on the state fair circuit?"

"Neither. After I accompany Dorothy back home to her family, I believe what I shall do is write up this little adventure in a book, Doctor. Much as you do the adventures of Mr. Holmes in *The Strand Magazine*," Frank Baum told us with a sly wink. "I have done some writing in my time, so I know I have the talent, and it appears to me that this should make a crackerjack of a story, and that it needs to be told."

"Oh, how wonderful!" Dorothy said with sheer joy. "And the Scarecrow, the Tin Man, and the Lion will all be in it?"

"Of course, little missy," Baum told us with a wide smile of joyful mirth.

"That will be wonderful!" Dorothy added happily.

"Well, we shall have plenty of time to recount it all on our long journey back to America, and to Kansas, Dorothy," Baum told my niece.

I nodded in agreement at that, but noted the dark look that now grew upon Holmes' face.

Frank Baum smiled indulgently when he noticed my friend's concern, "Fear not, Mr. Holmes, in my version of the Oz story, neither you, nor Doctor Watson shall ever appear. Not even a mention. I shall concentrate only on Dorothy's own story—on those events that happened *before* we ever appeared in Oz—but I think I will also change a few things here and there to make the events more of a children's story."

"I quite agree with you there, Mr. Baum," Holmes replied with a wry grin.

"Yes, I think it better that way—let people enjoy the story as a rather charming children's fantasy—and not leave any indication in my story that Oz is a real place and that it actually exists. After all, we do not want people going about searching for it, do we? I think not. So I shall write it as a fairy tale for children." Baum added giving us a sly wink. "However, I intend to do it right, so it may take me some time before the finished book appears in any case."

"Take all the time you need, Mr. Baum, in fact, I very much agree with you taking your time and that particular tack to the story," Holmes said now with a beaming smile of approval.

"On the other hand I may write it rather quickly," Baum replied with a wide grin, "while it is all fresh in my mind."

"I am sure no one would ever believe your story in any case should you write it as a serious travel journey, so making it a children's fairy tale should work quite well. What do you think, Watson, you are our resident scribe?"

"Absolutely, Holmes," I told my detective friend with a wide grin, "but I warn you both, I shall also write up my own version of this story some day—and it will be the actual story, or at least it shall tell the truth of our small part in it. Some day."

"Yes, some day, Watson, but not for some time, I think," Holmes said softly in deep thought. "I think there may be another chapter to add once we return to London."

I nodded wistfully, the true story might make a most unusual tale and I felt that it needed to be told. The fact that Oz was an actual place gave me much room for thought on how to approach our story. I knew it would be some time before I ever attempted such a fantastic chronicle, and I was certain, as Holmes stated—this story has not ended—not for us.

Meanwhile, our travel in the balloon did not take long, for we caught a brisk breeze that shot our vessel quickly across the sky. I felt like one of the heroes in Mr. Verne's fantastic novels, for in one of them he also proposed far away travel in a hot air balloon—an amazing trip of travel around the world, no less, that took only eighty days. Amazing! So balloon travel had much to commend it, even though I knew it could be most dangerous.

Frank Baum had set his controls well, set to a hair's breath accuracy I was sure with the help of the magic of Oz, and Holmes' own guidance based upon the work of Professor Challenger, so that the next morning we found ourselves gently flying over Central London.

"Ah, London! Home!" I gushed happily to see the magnificent city now sprawled out before us.

Holmes smiled, looked over at Frank Baum and quipped, "All our theories worked perfectly. Perhaps a meeting between yourself and Professor Challenger might be in order?"

Baum smiled grandly, "Can you arrange that?"

"It would be my pleasure. I am sure you two will have much to discuss regarding cyclones and violent weather patterns."

I now saw below us the wide lush pastures of Hyde Park. Mr. Baum pushed the control rod that guided our vessel downwards and soon our balloon descended gently upon the green grass of a wide pasture in the vast city parkland. It was early morning and the area at that hour was devoid of people.

"Well Watson, I think it is now fair to say that we are not in Oz anymore!" Holmes told me with a wan smile.

"Well, Holmes, as far as I am concerned, I am greatly relieved that I am finally home again in London!" I blurted out in sheer joy, my eyes taking in the familiar sights and sounds of our fair city that made my heart skip a beat. "It is certainly good to be back home where we belong. There is no place quite like it. Witch's and Winkies and flying monkeys not excepted! And Dorothy, you shall be home soon too!"

"I can not wait!" Dorothy replied happily.

"Yes, good old Watson, we have returned from a most interesting adventure. Had I not told you from the very outset of this venture that something always most interesting happens when I travel to America?"

"Yes, indeed you did, Holmes, and you were more than correct."

"Come now, let us head back to Baker Street, for I am famished and have been looking forward to some of Mrs. Hudson's excellent home cooking. Mr. Baum, you and Dorothy shall accompany us. I think I can promise you both a most tasty meal."

"Our housekeeper, is an outstanding cook, Mr. Baum—or should I just say, Frank? Come and enjoy it with us," I told the man I had known for so long as Professor Wonder, and my young niece.

"Frank is just fine with me, and that sounds wonderful, John," L. Frank Baum spoke up with great interest. I was sure he was as famished for some good English food as I was.

"Yes, Uncle John, that sounds utterly delightful," Dorothy said joyfully, and little Toto gave out with a sharp bark of approval.

Sherlock Holmes laughed joyfully, "Excellent! Then let us all be off to our rooms at Baker Street and what I expect will be a most satisfying evening of delicious food, good wine, and some fascinating conversation!"

I smiled back at Sherlock Holmes, our new friend, Frank, and my niece Dorothy, "Well, I am certainly with you there, for I am famished!"

"Good old Watson, always hungry! And you, Mr. Baum, and Dorothy are in for a real treat of stout English food," Holmes stated with a warm grin.

"I can not wait, Mr. Holmes, I have never been to London" said Frank, giving us a wide smile and a twitch of his mustache and bushy eyebrows.

"Nor I," Dorothy added with excitement.

"I am afraid London can not compare very much to Oz," Holmes told Dorothy confidentially, "but I am sure good old Watson will be happy to show you and Frank around before you start on your trip back to America."

"Of course, I would be most delighted," I answered happily.

"Well, no place can compare to Oz, Mr. Holmes, no place at all. However, some day I shall write my book about it and I hope to make the characters, and the magic of Oz come to life through the story in my book for all to encounter, as we did," L. Frank Baum replied with a happy grin, and all four of us gave knowing grins of mirth as we each recalled our own special memories of our recent adventure in the Magical Land of Oz.

CHAPTER 19: THE WONDERFUL WIZARD OF OZ

Sherlock Holmes allowed a deep look of satisfaction to cross his face that I had not often seen. We were in our rooms at Baker Street. He told me simply, "Well, all is well here in London. Lestrade, after getting over his shock and realization that Moriarty is alive, has things under control rounding up all of his associates regarding the Red Poppy Menace. It seems with the mirror portal destroyed, that has abruptly ended Moriarty's supply of that deadly drug to our world. Oscar has also promised to notify his brother Frank through the crystal orb should anything amiss come up that we should know about."

"That is certainly good news."

"Yes, it is ironic, that in the Witch's furious effort to destroy me with her lightning bolt—she destroyed the mirror and effectively put Moriarty out of business."

I nodded showing my relief, as I sifted through some newly delivered letters.

"Well, Watson, I see that the mail has come in. Anything of merit?" Holmes asked me curious as to what I was looking at.

"Yes, in fact I have the mail here, the usual bills of course, but we have a package from America! Why it is from Mr. Baum!"

"Well bring it here and open it straight away!" Holmes told me, not hiding his excitement, even as I could not hide my own. The package had some weight to it. I wondered what it could be?

I took out my pen knife and cut the string and tore the brown wrapping paper away.

"Holmes, there is a letter here, to me from my niece Dorothy. And a book, look at it!'

"I see it, Watson, *The Wonderful Wizard of Oz* by L. Frank Baum, the cover proclaims. Let me see it," Holmes asked and I handed him the book. It was new, just having been published and had some heft to it. He looked the book over most carefully.

Meanwhile, I concerned myself with the letter to me from Dorothy that Baum had enclosed in the package. I told Holmes, "It seems my niece is now back home in Kansas, in her new house with her Aunt Em and Uncle

Henry and all is well. Mr. Baum was as good as his word in helping her with her travel back home. She thanks us Holmes, for our help during her adventure in Oz. She said she shall never forget it, nor us."

I was sure that none of us would ever forget it either! Nor Dorothy!

"That is very well, Watson," Holmes mumbled, I could see he was busy looking over the book most intently.

"She also said she has sent back our valises of clothing and personal items we packed on our trip to Kansas, returning by steamship," I informed my friend.

"A most thoughtful young lady," Holmes quipped a bit distracted.

"So, I see you have some interest in the book?"

Holmes smiled nodding with approval, "You know, Mr. Denslow's depictions of Dorothy and her three companions on the cover seem most accurate, and look, Baum has even inscribed the book."

"How wonderful! What did he write?" I asked most curious.

Holmes held up the book, showing me the title page, then read what was written there, "'To Mr. Sherlock Holmes and Doctor John Watson, I hope you find this book of interest. Thank you for all your help, all best wishes, your friend in adventure, L. Frank Baum.' And there is a postscript, Watson, which adds, 'I am already at work on a sequel!'"

"That was most kind of him to sign and inscribe the book."

"Yes, it was. Well, Watson, it appears that I have my reading set for the evening. I am sure Frank's book shall prove most entertaining—as long as you and I are not mentioned anywhere within it! We must, after all, maintain our anonymity."

"Oh, Holmes, you know his book will be wonderful!"

"Yes, of course, but what I am really looking forward to reading some day is that book where you tell our own story of this strange little adventure."

"Yes, Holmes, some day, but for now read Frank's book, enjoy it, and when you finish it, I would like to give it a read."

"Fine, Watson, I am sure you will find it as delightful as will I!"

Then I spoke up in surprise, "Hello! What is this? Another letter?"

I certainly was not expecting this. Nor was my companion evidently.

My words immediately drew Holmes' rapt attention. "What does it say?"

"It is from Frank Baum," I stated, unfolding the single foolscap sheet.

"Of course it is, what does he say?"

"He says, 'My friends, by the way, I am making good use of the crystal globe the Winkie king gave me and I have named it Miranda II. I have made contact with my brother, Oscar, and all seems well in Oz, albeit, there is some minor problem concerning a missing rare black pearl, but not anything for you to worry about, I am sure.'"

"A rare missing black pearl?" I looked at my detective friend, "What do you think about that, Holmes?"

"I think, Watson, once more in Oz, the game shall be afoot!"

CHAPTER 20: OBSERVATIONS

While the events in this story have taken place in London and Oz in the latter years of the 18th Century, I have written of them contemporaneously. So this actual story was written many years later. With that in mind, I have included certain aspects of the story that have occurred in those later years, but that I feel show some connection between our world, and the world of Oz.

I remember, that at the time, Sherlock Holmes was looking into a connection between the supposed Andaman Islander, Tonga. With this in mind, he noted the American author Edgar Allan Poe and his fictional crime story "The Murders in the Rue Morgue". However, Poe's fictional story was based on a true account that happened years earlier regarding some kind of 'monkey criminal'—perhaps a baboon—that was trained to steal. Holmes saw some connection between this creature and Tonga, as well as a similar creature that was following him about London for some unknown reason. At the time he was not sure if these actions were connected to his problem of the Red Poppy Menace that was just then beginning to appear in London. We only learned later that Tonga was indeed a creature from Oz, in fact, he was a Munchkin that had turned bad, and that he had an evil younger brother by the name of Songa. These Munchkins were misshaped and twisted by their acceptance of evil and were used by the wicked Witch of the West to move between the worlds and do her bidding. I had killed Tonga, shot him dead, in the case I chronicled under the title, "The Sign of The Four", but at the time we never guessed that he had a younger brother. It was this younger brother, Songa, who transported the red poppy powder to Moriarty, through the use of the Witch's magical mirror.

A Doctor Presbury, and his experiments, are mentioned in this story. Years later, in 1903, now as Professor Presbury, he appeared in my friend's case that I chronicled as the story, "The Creeping Man". Presbury was found to be using an experimental monkey elixir of what he called "animal essence" which he thought gave him youth and power. Earlier, when just a young doctor, it seems he had experimented with various creatures, and through the use of a crystal ball and a magic mirror—who knows where he obtained these magical instruments—he exiled his winged experiments to Oz. Moriarty later found out about the crystal ball and the magic mirror, and stole them from Presbury, using them for his own purposes as he contacted the Witch of The West. Holmes having heard of Presbury's experiments with beasts, feared what it might lead to in the future. It was even possible that Robert Louis Stevenson had heard of Presbury's experiments, and it seems he may have used them as the basis for his book, *Dr. Jekyll and Mr. Hyde*.

While Holmes formed up his Baker Street Irregulars—his unofficial young detectives who helped him solve some cases first in "A Study in Scarlet", and last heard of in "The Adventure of the Crooked Man"— Holmes also used a small group of Munchkin children from Oz, who he also termed his Irregulars. These Munchkin Irregulars, led by a boy named Boq worked to help us in this case, much as their London counterparts did.

Holmes and I had never had a chance to meet Professor Edward Challenger up to the time of this story, however, we would meet the famed Professor and solve a case for him many years later that dealt with the national security and the *Titanic* tragedy. For information on that case, see "Challenger's Titanic Challenge" which has appeared in *Sherlock Holmes Mystery Magazine*.

While Holmes and I had dealt with a giant deadly hound in the case I chronicled as "The Hound of The Baskervilles", I had never encountered such a really, *really* enormous hound—that was invisible as well—as the beast we fought in the castle of the wicked Witch of the West. However, I believe it proves just one more link between our world and the Land of Oz. I am sure that there may be more connections between these two realms of existence. I leave it up to you, gentle reader, to find any other connections that may be apparent in the text of our story.

AUTHOR'S NOTE

Sherlock Holmes in Oz is based solely upon the original novel by L. Frank Baum, *The Wonderful Wizard of Oz*. Specifically, the Bobbs-Merrill hardcover edition of 1903, which reprints the original 1900 novel, with character descriptions based upon illustrations by W.W. Denslow from that original book. For my novel I have gone back to the original source material which is in the public domain. All descriptions and nomenclature is taken from that original first novel. I would like to acknowledge the assistance of my wife, and illustrator, Lucille Cali, in the creation of this book. Her help was crucial. I hope you enjoy this book as much as I did in writing it.

ABOUT THE AUTHOR

Gary Lovisi is a Mystery Writers of America, Edgar Award Nominated author for his Sherlock Holmes pastiche story, "The Adventure of The Missing Detective." He has written numerous Sherlock Holmes pastiches, and non-fiction articles. He has written for *Sherlock Holmes Mystery Magazine*, (including the Holmes / Challenger team-up story, "Challengers Titanic Challenge" that appeared in issue #12 in 2014); as well as three anthologies from St. Martin's Press, edited by Michael Kurland. His story, "The American Adventure" chronicles the early travels of a young Holmes with Dr. Joseph Bell to America. He has also written *Sherlock Holmes: The Baron's Revenge* (Airpship27, 2012) which is a sequel to the original Holmes story by Doyle, "The Illustrious Client". Lovisi has also written three books in *The Secret Adventures of Sherlock Homes* series (Ramble House Books), and his Inspector Mac and Holmes team-up adventures in Stark House Press's Black Gat Book #11 in 2017. You can find out more about Lovisi and his work at his website: www.gryphonbooks.com and through his page at Facebook. Also check out his *Youtube* videos on all kinds of collectable books.

www.ingramcontent.com/pod-product-compliance
Lightning Source LLC
Chambersburg PA
CBHW020654180626
46816CB00003B/1272